"The television an...
continued. "I'll c... two in her book
just to see what they know about her, but one of
them was in New York and the other was in the
hospital."

"All men?" Salter questioned.

"All the ones in the book."

They had now cleared the groundwork. There was
only one question left. Salter asked it: "So who was
with her that afternoon?"

"The guy who killed her, I would think. All we know
is, he's called 'Abe.' They drank some wine, then he
killed her."

"Let's find Abe. Ask him. Any ideas?"

"Not yet. I have to put everything I've got through
a sieve, find out what these people are lying about."

"Who?"

"All of them."

★

"Charlie Salter is in top form."
    —*Washington Post Book World*

**"A Sensitive Case seems certain to add further
members to the Charlie Salter fan club."**
    —*Books in Canada*

A *Forthcoming Worldwide Mystery by*
ERIC WRIGHT

FINAL CUT

Also available from Worldwide Mystery by
ERIC WRIGHT

A QUESTION OF MURDER

A SENSITIVE CASE
ERIC WRIGHT

WORLDWIDE

TORONTO · NEW YORK · LONDON · PARIS
AMSTERDAM · STOCKHOLM · HAMBURG
ATHENS · MILAN · TOKYO · SYDNEY

A SENSITIVE CASE

A Worldwide Mystery/November 1991

This edition is reprinted by arrangement with Charles Scribner's Sons, an imprint of Macmillan Publishing Company.

ISBN 0-373-26083-0

Printed in U.S.A.

For Gladys Brown

ONE

"WHAT'S THIS?" Sergeant Pickett held up the note between thumb and forefinger and waved it in the direction of the temporary supervisor of the Bail and Parole Unit, Staff Sergeant "Call Me Taffy" Williams.

"Just what it says, Mel, boy. They want you to help out in Special Affairs. Shorthanded, they are."

Alda, one of the civilians, laughed. "They think we are sitting around here doing our knitting."

"What's 'Special Affairs'? Is it a unit?" Pickett asked.

"A center, they call it. It was set up a couple of years ago to handle anything out of the way." Williams spoke over a plywood partition that separated his head from the rest of his body. He had popped up to find out why Pickett was late that morning.

The Bail and Parole Unit was housed in the basement of 51 Division, on Regent Street, in the heart of the oldest working-class district in Toronto. The unit occupied a space about the size of a four-car garage. In the corner of the room opposite Williams, a lineup of bailees and parolees waited at a counter to report their presence; as many as six hundred appeared in a day. Williams was partitioned off in one corner; eight other desks shared the rest of the space. Half a dozen sergeants staffed the unit, mainly older men who had once worked in Homicide or the Holdup Squad or the Investigation Branch. They had come to the Bail and Parole Unit to wind down their careers quietly, away from the stress of responding to alarms at night. They worked regular hours in two daytime shifts, usually in the office, with an occasional excursion to look for a defector who failed to report. Their value to the unit was that collectively they knew by sight nearly every minor criminal in Toronto.

Sergeant Pickett had joined the force in the days when size was the most important criterion (a qualification that was now creating some problems in the drive to recruit officers from the ethnic minorities). He had softened only slightly with age, shifting from burly to just solid. Short white hair, dressed in a blue serge suit, he looked what he almost was, a retired detective wearing out his plain clothes. He glanced at the note again. "It says 'Homicide.' What's so out of the way about that?"

Williams' head floated above the partition. "Ah, well, you see, Homicide are shorthanded, too, so they passed it on to Special Affairs. They were the ones who passed it on to us, see. Why don't you go along and find out?"

Pickett looked across the room at another sergeant, seated by the door. "What's with Homicide, Dan? Why are they shorthanded? That was standard in my day."

Before Sergeant Danilo Marinelli could reply, Williams' head cut in. "Everybody is, Mel. Everybloodybody. Bloody great rash of resignations there's been, see, ever since Woodhouse and Baker got it in the neck."

Pickett nodded. Woodhouse and Baker were two detective sergeants who had resigned a month previously. They had spent a year on the trail of three killers, but when they got them at last before a judge the killers were released because the evidence against them was tainted; it had been obtained by means of an illegal wiretap, acquired under a pretext that the defending lawyer had shown to be false. The two detectives were isolated for purposes of laying blame and demoted, not by being reduced in rank but by being shifted to other duties. They did not make a fuss, even though they had acted throughout with the silent consent of their superiors. They had been caught behaving illegally and they were scapegoated. Those were the rules.

"That's two. Who else?"

"George Soper and Fred Yeo are on suspension," Marinelli offered.

"What for?"

"Alleged to have assaulted suspects," Marinelli said in a mock courtroom voice. "Ever since that rookie was convicted of assault last year you have to wear white gloves when you're handling a rounder."

"That's just the tip of the iceberg," Williams' head said, then, liking it, said it again. "Just the tip of the iceberg. There's been a lot more. You can't lift a finger now, boy, or the civilians will jump on your neck.''

There was a bark of laughter from the lineup at the end of the room. The two sergeants looked up, but the five faces behind the counter were already blank. Pickett continued to ponder the note.

Marinelli walked over to his desk. ''You hear about the guy handing out parking tickets last week? This yuppie comes along and starts screaming at him he's only parked his BMW there for about two minutes. Our guy keeps very cool, just explains to him he can't leave his toys in the street during the rush hour. The yuppie complains and our guy gets a reprimand for using derogatory language. Insulting him, like. So he quit.''

''Get on your horse now, Mel,'' Williams ordered. ''I told them you'd be there an hour ago. What kept you this morning, anyway?''

Pickett, who had come out of the house that morning to find not one but two flat tires, but disliked being called to account within the hearing of half a dozen minor criminals, said, ''I missed the ferry,'' knowing that Williams knew that he lived nowhere near the lake. He pointed at the work on his desk. ''What about this lot?''

''I'll find someone to pick up the slack. Don't worry about it.'' Williams looked sharply around the room at the forces under his command.

Still Pickett did not move. ''You know anything about 'Special Affairs,' Dan?''

Marinelli thought about the question. "They worked on a case once when I was in Homicide."

"What was special about that one?"

"Nothing. I'm trying to remember. There was an inspector involved whose wife was a politico. His first wife, that was it. Threatening to make a fuss because we hadn't caught a rapist. Feminist."

"What happened?"

"We caught the guy. *He* caught the guy. The inspector. Salter, his name was."

"Staff Inspector Salter is in charge of the center now," Williams' head said loudly, almost shouting. "He took over last year. He's waiting for you now in his office."

Pickett gave the supervisor a glance. "I haven't decided to go yet." He turned back to an amused Marinelli. "What's the guy like?"

"He didn't try to walk over us, and he let us take credit for the pinch. Want me to find out? I could give one of the boys a call. Wycke was pretty friendly with Salter, I think."

Pickett shook his head. "Don't bother." He turned back to Williams. "What was his old superintendent's name? The guy who used to run the center?"

"Orliff. Staff Superintendent Orliff. For God's sake, man, cut along now."

"In a minute." Pickett left the room and walked along the corridor until he found an empty office with a telephone. He dialed a number from a list he dug out of his wallet. When he got through he explained himself and his concern. Who was Salter? What was he like to work for?

He listened for a while, thanked his source, and hung up. He stayed in the empty office for a few minutes to think. A homicide involving a round-the-clock investigation would be bad news. On the other hand, what he had just heard about Salter sounded okay, and this case had already gone into its second stage, so it would probably not keep him away from home at night. He decided he might as well hear about it, at least.

Pickett was a widower, and it was a reasonable assumption by his colleagues that he continued working because he was afraid of the lonely desert that stretched in front of him. In fact, five years after his wife's death, he did not have enough time to do all he wanted. He was about to retire; the right moment would come when his work interfered with his private life. For Pickett the right to retire, the knowledge that he could retire at any time (a week's notice was enough) was like a bag of gold under the bed. That it was there and could be spent at any time gave him as much pleasure as spending it would have done: It increased the pleasure of working.

After his wife died, he had converted his small two-story-and-basement house into two apartments, and he rented out the second floor, keeping the ground floor for himself. He was planning to build a deck and a new garage, projects that would keep him busy for months. He read a lot, and for company he played poker once a week and ate supper at the home of one or other of his colleagues about as often. Finally, he had a secret, known only to his neighbor: He had started to build a log cabin on a patch of land about three hours north of Toronto, and he was looking forward to getting up there as soon as the access road dried out. He had no children; his only relatives were a sister-in-law (whom Pickett acknowledged to his cronies was a pain in the ass) and her son, his nephew. But they lived in Hamilton, an hour and a half away, and he didn't see enough of them to bother him much. These relatives apart, his life was satisfying and full, and any new assignment caused him to balance the pleasures of working against the rapidly-growing-level pleasures of not working. A major new learning experience might just tip the scales and cause him to reach for the bag of gold.

He returned to the office and put on his jacket. "I'll see what he wants," he said. He took his raincoat off the peg. "I'd better take this, too. See you, Dan." He looked across the room at the supervisor, who was still watching, waiting. "See you, Taffy," he said.

"Cheerio, Mel, boy. Good luck to you. Don't forget us, now. Let's know what's happening, will you?"

Marinelli followed Pickett out onto Regent Street. "See?" he said. "Just a kind word, that's all he wants. He's not *bad*. Just a silly bugger they've stuck us with until Bill Hart gets out of hospital. Don't let him put you off coming back."

Pickett sighed. "I know. He'll be gone in a week. Funny how hard it is, though. I did call him Taffy. Did you notice?"

He looked at his watch and tried to remember if there was a hardware store on any of the streets on his route north. Then he thought of Staff Sergeant Williams and put the idea away. Williams, he could be sure, would already be on the phone to say that he, Williams, had done his job and that Pickett was on his way. He had better get on with it and hope for a gap later in the day.

WHILE PICKETT WAS deciding that his routine was not going to be threatened by this new assignment, a very different threat was forming in the Public Affairs Unit, a few yards from where he was to meet Salter. A young girl was making inquiries at the front desk. She was trying to locate a police officer in his early sixties, perhaps retired. She didn't know his name or what he looked like, but she knew a great deal about his early life. She would not say why she was inquiring. It was a personal matter, she said.

The police constable wrote down the details she gave him, and guessing that "personal" might mean a problem, told her to come back the next day. He took the inquiry in to the inspector in charge of the unit, who agreed with him.

"When she comes back, tell her to write a letter. Tell her we only deal with personal inquiries in writing."

"Who should she address it to? Us?"

"Not *us,* no. We're Public Affairs. This is a private matter. The chief, of course. All requests for information should go to the chief. Didn't you know that?"

TWO

STAFF INSPECTOR Charlie Salter, newly appointed head of the Special Affairs Center, sat waiting for Pickett to arrive so that he could turn the case over to him and get on with the rest of his work. When Staff Superintendent Orliff retired, and Salter, lightly promoted, was given his job, he did not get a replacement for himself. A few weeks later his sergeant retired and Salter did not get a replacement for him, either, so that when the homicide case landed on his desk he was entirely on his own; *he* was the center. To an outsider it might have seemed that the center itself and Salter's job were at risk, but Salter knew that the opposite was true. It had been explained to him by his own supervisor that he had been promoted and not replaced to cut costs, but the center was an essential item in someone's budget because it still attracted its original allocation of funds, some of which could now be diverted. The center was a very valuable item if used creatively by a good budget manager.

At the moment Salter was working on an internal problem. The Police Commission had decided that the unusual number of resignations meant that morale in the force must be low. (They had been led to this idea by a series of articles in a Toronto newspaper. The series was titled "Toronto: A City in Decline," and one of the articles was critical of the police.) They set up an inquiry. A psychological consultant was hired, and Salter was assigned to help him. The man had spent a week in Salter's office asking the staff inspector questions as he went about his first task of designing a questionnaire with yes/no answers, the results of which could be tabulated on a computer. Salter's job, as he saw it, was to pretest the questions, to point out which were unanswerable or just silly. The section on alcoholism, for example ("Do you use alcohol? If so, regularly? Every day?"), led to the conclusion that a man who drank a bottle of beer every day when he got home was an alcoholic. It was taking all of Salter's time. The psychologist was poised nearby, waiting for another day's work, and Salter was holding him off until he could give Pickett his orders.

The case seemed routine enough. A woman had been found dead in her bathtub. She had not been dead long when the janitor let himself into her apartment. When she had not answered his knock, he assumed she was out, but he had been promising to fix the radiator in her living room for three weeks. The water was still warm, he told them later; except that she had her bathrobe on, she might just have stepped into the tub that second.

After the body was taken away, the first squad car stayed on the scene to keep the curious away, and two sergeants from Homicide began their inquiries. The immediate area was searched (when a killing is unpremeditated, the killer will usually run away as far as he can, but sometimes he will hide under the stairs, wondering what to do next); then the two sergeants began looking for witnesses who might have seen anyone running or driving away from the building.

No such witnesses were found, and so the secondary investigation began, the search for a suspect in the woman's world, someone with a motive for killing her, or for a thief whom she had surprised. After two days of inquiries the investigation became sensitive as the detectives found themselves checking up on a provincial deputy minister. They called at his office, looking, in their matching raincoats, exactly what they were, and the deputy minister was outraged at being treated like any ordinary suspect citizen. He put on a lot of pressure, both to have his relationship with the case dealt with discreetly and to have the two sergeants taken off it. At any other time he would have been wasting his influence, but Homicide, shorthanded like everyone else, jumped at the chance to unload the case, and it was passed to the Special Affairs Center, the proper place for sensitive matters.

A call to Harry Wycke, Salter's contact in Homicide, got the response that Pickett was a good man but hadn't worked on a homicide case for several years. Wycke was interested that he was still working at all.

"Anything I ought to know about him?" Salter asked.

"When he's irritated he can turn bolshie. Is that the word I want? There are a few stories about him. You know the kind: 'Did you hear what Mel said when the lawyer asked him in court how could he be sure that he had the right man, just because he caught him on the roof with a shotgun? Pickett said he deduced it. How? the lawyer wanted to know. Mel said the hunting season was over for the year. South of Bloor Street, that is.' Stuff like that. Ask a silly question and you'll get a silly answer. He doesn't like stupid orders, either. He was the guy who streaked the police dance in the sixties when that craze was on. Just because we all got a memo from the chief reminding us we had to be suitably dressed. Mel wore a paper sack over his head and a 'Do Not Disturb' sign, the kind hotels give you to hang on your doorknob. The chief decided to find it funny, but it didn't help when promotion time came around. He's had a couple of reprimands, so watch him. But don't let him catch you watching him unless you want to solve the case by yourself, which would be a pity because he's a better homicide man than you are.''

SALTER'S PHONE BUZZED to announce that Pickett was in the building, and a few moments later the sergeant stood in the doorway waiting, without nervousness, for Salter to wave him in.

Salter leaned across the desk to shake hands and pointed to a chair. A face looked around the corner. "I need about half an hour," Salter said over Pickett's shoulder. "I'll give you a shout." The telephone buzzed and Salter picked it up. "No calls for another half hour," he said before the operator could say anything. He turned to Pickett. "Shut the door, would you?"

As Pickett moved to the door, a uniformed constable appeared with a note, which Pickett handed on to Salter. The staff inspector read it and put it aside. "Christ," he said, "now I'm the Missing Persons Bureau. Let's start before anyone else comes in."

Pickett sat down, wondering if this was the moment come at last to tell them all to stuff it and to head for the woods. He remembered Salter now, though he had never worked with him. He was ten years younger than Pickett and about seventy-five pounds lighter, dressed in a reassuringly nondescript way without too much concern for his appearance, neither smart in a parade-ground way nor trendy like some of the new ones. His hair was longer than Pickett's and still brownish, but otherwise the two men were cast in similar molds. All this was reassuring enough; there should be no trouble getting along with him. What was bothering Pickett slightly was that Salter seemed to be under more of a strain than the extra work should account for. Where was all the stress coming from? Was Salter the kind who panicked if he had to do two things at once? Pickett had had experience with one or two of those. A bit of extra load and it was like working in the war room of the Pentagon. No thanks. Pickett settled himself warily in his chair, mentally fingering his resignation.

"Want some coffee?" Salter asked.

A good first sign. No "Sergeant," but no bon-homie, either. Pickett, too, laid aside Salter's rank, ready to pick it up if he was wrong, but seeing no cof-feepot in the office declined the offer, because al-though it was made without preamble and therefore probably genuine, if they had to wait while Salter sent out for coffee it might muddy the simplicity of this first contact.

He shook his head. "I just had some."

Salter nodded, drank a mouthful of his own, and moved the cup to a far corner of the desk.

"What happened to all the paper?" Pickett asked, suddenly. He pointed to the desk, which was bare ex-cept for a red file folder, two pencils, a pad of yellow lined paper, and the recently arrived note.

"The paper?"

"This was Orliff's office, wasn't it?"

"That's right. He's retired. It's mine now."

"So what did you do with the paper?"

"Ah." Comprehension broke through. The paper. The piles of paper that Orliff used to keep in neat stacks around the edge of the desk. Salter pointed be-hind him to where Orliff's papers sat in a single pile on a shelf, interleaved with a dozen markers. "I filed them. Did you know Orliff?"

"A bit. We joined together."

"You still talk to him?"

"Once in a while."

"Lately?"

Pickett considered his reply. Salter wasn't making conversation. He wanted to know if Pickett and Salter's old boss were buddies. "I spoke to him this morning."

Salter nodded. "How is he?"

"Fine. Waiting to get up to his cottage." He watched Salter taking it in. Now Salter knew that Pickett had checked him out.

"You know what this case is all about?"

"It's a homicide, I heard. How'd it land up here?"

"Homicide have their hands full. That and a little bit of sensitivity. Some important people are involved. One, anyway. The woman called herself a massage therapist, and she had a couple of well-known clients."

"One of those?" Pickett's tone conveyed a request for information, not a judgment.

"According to the janitor's wife, yes. According to the clients Homicide spoke to, no. We'll have to find that out. Homicide interviewed everyone they could find, but there was someone else there that afternoon, just before she died, a client, whom they haven't found. He's the most likely suspect. Here." Salter passed the file over the desk.

"Why me?" Pickett took the file without opening it.

Salter spread his hands, sharing the sergeant's question. "I've got an internal investigation and a lot of other stuff, and I asked for some help. My sergeant quit and I haven't got a replacement. Right now I'm on my own. You were recommended."

"Who by?"

"Wycke, in Homicide."

Now Pickett knew that Salter had checked *him* out. He made a mental note to find out who Salter's sergeant was and why he had quit. So far, he approved of what he had seen of Salter, but he didn't want any surprises.

"Sergeant Gatenby left because he'd developed a heart problem," Salter said. "He wanted to stay on but they told him he couldn't. He comes by from time to time. I'll introduce him."

"You have to wonder why," Pickett said, smiling slightly.

"Sure you do. So ask around. Now, why you? I didn't ask for you. I asked for someone who knew how to run a homicide investigation. This isn't a dangerous job. Just a little tricky. You *were* in Homicide?"

"Until three years ago. I got too old and I didn't want to retire so they found me a chair in Bail and Parole." Pickett looked around the room, a fairly large one but with only one desk. "Do I work out of this office?"

"You can have the room next door."

"I report just to you, or to Homicide, or what?"

"Just to me."

Pickett moved his chair slightly to sit square to the desk and placed the file in front of him. "Can we start now?"

"Have you seen the apartment?"

"I was over there this morning, first thing."

"What's it like in there? What kind of place did she have?"

"Don't you plan to take a look yourself?"

"I'm going over right away, soon as we're through. I thought you might give me something to suck on before I got there. Did it seem like a whore's apartment?"

"No, it didn't. It looked like your average apartment of a single woman with a good income. Nice furniture, pictures, lots of kitchen equipment, lots of cookbooks, lots of every kind of books. But that's all in the file. Pictures, too."

"No kinky stuff around?"

"None."

"Cash? A hundred dollars a trick soon turns into a drawerful."

"Just what was in her wallet."

"And these sensitive guys. Who are they?"

"They're in the file. One's a deputy minister in the provincial government. A whiz kid, they tell me. He's breathing very heavy."

"All civil servants shit bricks when we come around. The higher they are, the bigger the bricks. Rumors start flying, and then the reporters start sniffing around. They've always got something to hide, those guys. Who's the other one?"

"He's a TV host on one of those investigative-type shows. He seems very cooperative. Homicide says he's too cooperative, and they were very careful with him in case they wound up on his show."

"But he's not shouting that his privacy is being invaded?"

"Apparently not. We're the ones being sensitive. Which makes me think that the girl *was* a masseuse and there's nothing for anyone to get uptight about."

"Then why this deputy minister getting hysterical? If she wasn't on the game, that is."

"Because of how it could look. Everybody wonders what kind of massage he might be into."

Pickett opened the file and glanced at the first two pages. "I'll have to talk to him. He cut the Homicide guys off."

"Sure, but I'll phone him first and make the arrangements."

Pickett continued reading. "What about this janitor and his wife? What did you make of them?"

"Name's Turnow. He's about forty. Big guy. Bit of a blowhard. The kind who makes a production out of everything. Sees himself as working day and night, trying to keep up with the impossible. When I was there, one of the tenants asked him to look at a tap. She'd asked him before—more than once, from the sound of it. 'I'll get to it as soon as I can,' he said. It sounded like his theme song. His wife is a couple of years older than him, I would guess. She claims the girl was a tart. Her husband said he was too busy to notice."

Pickett laughed. "Now I can read the file. Am I on my own?"

"There was a detective, Constable Metella, checking the block. She'll report to you today, but you'll

have to take over the questioning. She's been reas-
signed.''

"She?"

"That's right. I think this was her first job."

"Well, well," Pickett said. He stood up. "I'll read
the file and go over there this morning. I wouldn't
mind some coffee now. Where do I get it?"

"Public Affairs. They have a kitty, but they'll sell
you a cup for fifty cents. They'll lend you a mug."

Pickett left, and Salter returned to trying to concentrate on a psychologist's questions. At some time,
he knew, he would have to find a space to talk to the
sergeant, ask him about himself, welcome him aboard,
as it were, even for a short trip. But not right now.
Right now, and for the past twenty-four hours, he had
been doing his job with about a quarter of his brain,
leaving no room for courtesy, while the remaining
three-quarters of his brain tried to think about what he
was going to do about the fact that Annie, his wife,
seemed to be having an affair.

Salter knew himself to be extremely vulnerable. The
idea of an involvement of her and someone else was
unthinkable; if true, shattering. Under the circum-
stances, he had done well to deal with Pickett as if it
were a normal, if cheerless, day. If he could keep the
psychologist chained up he might have time to think,
or at least to get used to the idea.

THREE

THE STORY IN THE FILE was essentially what Pickett had heard from Salter, with the addition of the preliminary investigation. The woman's name was Linda Thomas. Her passport photo showed a thin, dark-haired woman who carried her head forward with an air of curiosity, smiling cautiously. She was forty-two. She had been found by the janitor in her tub, still wearing her bathrobe. There was a contusion on the back of her head and a matching indentation in the wall of her living room. Apparently she had been slammed against the wall, then dragged into the bathroom and dumped into the tub, which she had probably just filled for herself before the killer arrived. The door to the balcony was ajar; access from the parking lot onto the balcony was easy at this level. The front door was closed but not chained. There was no sign of a struggle except for the bruises around her neck where she had been grabbed. According to the pathologist, the blow on her head had been sufficient to kill her.

She had been a good housekeeper, and very few prints had survived her cleaning. Most of the ones the experts found were her own. The exceptions were a set on the bottle of wine, still on the coffee table, and a good single print on the visitor's wineglass. The neighbors had been questioned, but so far no one had been found who heard any shouts or screams. Pickett read the file through and went to work.

THE APARTMENT BLOCK was on Abercrombie Boulevard off Victoria Park Avenue, near where it meets Eglinton Avenue. It was typical of its time, lacking any architectural grace, but not a monstrosity. What saved it was that land in the fifties in this part of Toronto was still cheap enough to allow for a bit of landscaping. The building was set well back from the boulevard, far enough to allow for a large ornamental garden in front with half a dozen good-sized trees, a fountain that jetted two stories high, and a fringe of red and white flowers. A drive curved around this garden in front of the main entrance, which was overhung by a concrete awning.

Pickett left his car on the street and walked behind the building where, as Salter had told him, he found the sign for Tuck Shop—a tiny general store in the basement. The security consisted of a sign inviting customers of the store to press the buzzer to gain access. Pickett pressed the buzzer, the door clicked, and he was inside, unidentified and free to wander at will. Just in case any attempt at a check was kept, he followed the signs to the shop, bought a newspaper, and made a show of looking for something on the shelves. While he was in the store, the buzzer sounded three times without any more customers appearing, and Pickett was satisfied that as long as the Tuck Shop was open, anyone had access to the building without fear of being intercepted.

The janitor's apartment was on the same level, but at the other end of the corridor from the Tuck Shop. On the door, a huge notice told the tenants when the janitor was available, warning them not to disturb him at other times. The bullying tone of the notice indicated how much easier tenants were to find than janitors. A sign of the times.

Pickett banged on the door and was shouted at unintelligibly, from inside. He banged again, harder this time, and the door opened on a slightly overweight man in early middle age, wearing a singlet and Bermuda shorts.

"What's the matter with you people?" he asked as he appeared in the doorway. "Can't you read? I don't work in the mornings. It's eleven-thirty. If you want me, come back later, or leave a message in the envelope on the door."

Pickett waited for him to finish, then showed his card.

"Oh, Jesus. You again? Look, chief, I've got work to do. I've told you guys everything that happened."

"Who is it, Larry?" a woman's voice called from within.

"Police!" he shouted over his shoulder, keeping his eyes on Pickett. "Again!"

The woman appeared beside her husband. She looked, as Salter had said, a few years older than he. A clean-looking, bony face, without makeup, short-haired, with a brown woolen dress and bare white legs ending in pink woolen foot warmers. She was smoking a cigarette, clasping and unclasping her wrist between puffs.

Pickett waited to be invited in, but when the couple continued to stand in the doorway, he retreated a pace. "I've got a few questions I'd like to ask you," he said loudly. "About the woman who was drowned, about what you know of the tenants, and about the security arrangements in this block."

A door opened along the corridor and a white-haired lady looked out. Pickett nodded to her, and the janitor's wife stepped out into the corridor to see who he was acknowledging. "It's all right, dear," she called. Then, to Pickett, "You'd better come inside. I hope this won't take as long as last time."

The apartment was clean and well kept, but it looked as if it was furnished with the abandoned effects of departed tenants. In one corner a television set was broadcasting a game show. Around it in a ring that took up most of the rest of the space were four old mismatched armchairs. The woman closed off the door to the bedroom and pulled a rattan curtain across the doorway to the kitchen. She gestured Pickett to sit down, pulling her husband down in the chair next to her. When the janitor started to speak, she motioned him to silence and the two of them waited for Pickett to begin.

"Let's start again," he said. "Tell me how you found the body, what time, what you were doing in the apartment."

"We've been through all this," the janitor began, and once more his wife shushed him. Pickett waited. Finally the man began again, his voice weary, self-pitying. "At half past five on Friday afternoon I went over to her apartment to have a look at her radiator. She'd been complaining about the cold because she said the radiator in her bedroom wasn't working properly."

"When did she complain?"

"About a week before. I tried to get to it sooner, but a place like this, you're at everyone's beck and call. I've got my hands full. Always somebody wants something. One guy can't keep up."

"Did you knock?"

"I knocked and pressed the buzzer three or four times. Finally I let myself in and found her there in the tub. I pulled her out—she was heavy as hell—and laid her on the floor, but I didn't know what to do with her, so I ran out and got Bonnie, who came back with me and tried to revive her while I called the police. Then they came and took her away."

"Why did you go and look at her radiator at five-thirty? The sign on your door says you're not on call after five."

"I told you, I have to work all the hours God gave me to keep up. Besides, I didn't want her bothering me on my weekend."

"She bug you a lot, did she?" Pickett asked in a commiserating voice.

Turnow opened his mouth wide, closed it with a sharp click, and looked hard at his left foot. "Not more than most. They all think the sign's not for them."

"She ever bother you outside your proper working hours? Apart from leaving you notes?"

This time Turnow consulted the television set and looked at his wife before replying. "No, I suppose not. She wasn't as bad as some."

"You got a master key for getting into the apartments when the tenants are out?"

"I never go in when they're not there. Never. Unless they give me proper permission or it's an emergency. Never."

"But you can."

"I have the right, yes. I'm the owner's agent. When it's necessary. For emergencies."

"We have to be able to get in for emergencies," his wife said.

"Sure. She give you permission?"

"She left notes. That's as good as, isn't it?"

"How many? How many notes did she leave you?" The previous two weeks had been bitterly cold as Toronto inched toward spring. A faulty radiator was serious.

"Just a couple. I got to it as soon as I could."

"Where else were you working that afternoon? Who saw you?"

"No one. I was having a nap here—I'd been up late the night before. There was a lot of noise in the parking lot behind. I'm responsible for everything here. Why?"

"He was asleep when I came home from work at two. He didn't leave the apartment all afternoon. I can testify to that," his wife said.

Pickett looked at her, waiting for her to continue.

"I don't usually come home until six," she said. "But I had a headache that day and came back early. Larry woke up about four-thirty and went down to the boiler room to get his tools while I made us a cup of tea."

"You said he didn't leave the apartment all afternoon?"

"Just to get his tools."

"I was only gone a minute."

"Let me get this straight," Pickett said. "I work for a real stickler, and if he sees anything I haven't covered, he can get very nasty. Now, you were in the apartment all afternoon except that you went out once, just after four-thirty, and you went down to the boiler room. Then you had a cup of tea. Then, around five-thirty, you went over to her apartment. That right? Have I got it straight?" Help me out, his attitude said.

"That's it, chief," Turnow said. "You got it." He exchanged agreeing smiles with his wife.

"Did you get any calls in the afternoon?"

"Two or three people came to the door," his wife answered. "The phone rang once, I think. I didn't answer any of them. I'm not at their beck and call. He's the janitor, not me." She lit another cigarette and put the match in her pocket.

"And you stayed here all afternoon?"

"I slipped out once to get some milk at the Tuck Shop."

"What time was that?"

"About four."

"Did you see anyone on the way? In the corridor, near the apartment?"

"Mrs. Boychuck, across the hall. The one who poked her head out to you. She tried to catch me about her stove when she heard my door open. One of the burners is gone. She'll remember."

"And that was it?"

"That's right. We had a cup of tea and then Larry decided he'd better look at the radiator. That's when he found her."

Pickett walked over to the front door and looked through the peephole, noting the section of the corridor that could be seen. "Show me around, would you, Mr. Turnow? If you've got time, that is."

Turnow missed Pickett's mockery, but his wife looked at him sharply. "Sure," Turnow said. "What do you want to see?"

"Bring your keys." Pickett turned to the janitor's wife. "Thanks, Mrs. Turnow. Where do you work, by the way? In case I need to find you."

"I'm a waitress in Zooey's on Yonge Street. I work days, Tuesday to Saturday."

Pickett nodded and stepped out into the corridor with Turnow. "Where to, chief?" Turnow asked, jauntily.

"Let's start in the boiler room. Which way?"

"Why? What do you want to go down there for? There's nothing down there."

"Down this way?" Pickett stood back to let Turnow lead the way. They walked to the end of the corridor, where the janitor pushed open the fire door into the basement and opened the door of the furnace room. He put his hand around the jamb to switch on the light. "See? It's just a furnace room. What are you looking for?"

Pickett walked past the janitor, ignoring the question, past the furnace to the space beyond, an area about eight feet square behind the boiler, containing an armchair with a torn seat cushion and a wooden apple box standing on end to serve as a table. A copy of *Penthouse* on the apple box completed the sense of a den. Pickett sat down in the armchair and picked up the magazine while Turnow watched. He looked around the dim little nest and saw the bottle of Canadian Port behind the shovel. It was about a quarter full. Beside it was a plastic tumbler.

"This your workroom?"

"It's my little hideaway." The janitor made a sound between a hiss and a giggle. "I get those out of the tenants' garbage and sometimes I take a little break down here. I got a whole stack of them, right there in the box.''

The secret life of Larry Turnow, Pickett thought. Reading *Penthouse* and drinking Canadian Port under a forty-watt bulb in a hole heated to ninety degrees. He studied the stapled parts of the centerfold, then dropped the magazine to the floor and led Turnow back into the main corridor of the basement and up the stairs. Turnow passed him as they emerged onto the floor above and stepped forward to open the door of the dead woman's apartment.

"Leave it," Pickett said. "Who lives here?" He pointed to the door almost opposite.

"She's some kind of writer. Works for a magazine. She's away right now, been away for a month. In Europe somewhere."

"When does she get back?"

Turnow shook his head. "She doesn't tell us when she's going or when she's coming back. The other guy already looked in there."

Pickett continued down the hall. "Who lives here?"

"That's Mrs. Boychuck's place."

The only other apartment in that half of the corridor was Turnow's. Pickett considered the area for a few moments. "Let me have the master key, will you? I want to spend some time in the apartment."

"I have to come with you."

"I'll bring you the key when I'm through."

"I'm not supposed to let the key out of my possession. I could let you in, though, and you could close up after you come out."

Pickett held out his hand like a parent, ignoring Turnow's reluctance. The janitor sighed, shrugged, took the key off the ring, and gave it to Pickett. "I should get some kind of receipt," he said.

"I'll bring it back within the hour." He returned to the dead woman's apartment, taking his time, waiting for Turnow to shut his door.

Inside the apartment, Pickett sat down and waited for the impressions to come. The first was of a greenhouse, full of extremely uninteresting plants. There were pots hanging from the ceiling, ranged along the windowsills and on most of the other surfaces in the room, all of them sporting or trailing greenery, none of which was in bloom. It was like a giant aquarium from which the water had been drained. He walked into the bedroom and found that the featured plant was cactus, ugly and spiky, designed by nature to look unappetizing but here cultivated for its beauty. The apartment was otherwise conventionally and sensibly furnished from the middle range of a department store, including a couch that converted into a pull-out bed. There was a print of flowers in the center of each wall, each one part of a series; there was a shelf of crime novels, another of books on drugless medicine—chiropractic, massage, homeopathy, herbs—and three other shelves of paperback fiction. A glass-fronted cabinet held a collection of small jugs, a few wineglasses, and a single bottle of sweet vermouth. On a coffee table there was a space among half a dozen pots of plants, a space where the bottle of wine and two glasses had been.

Pickett glanced briefly around the bathroom and looked out at the balcony. The bedroom was next, her workplace. One end of it was an office with an electric typewriter; a filing cabinet; and two small shelves containing a dictionary and some office supplies—scissors, envelopes, typing paper. In the center of the room was the massage table, and in the corner a wire-mesh container of clean sheets. A shelf beside the container held several plastic bottles of a medical-looking nature. Pickett pulled back the heavy drapes over the windows and found a set of closed venetian blinds. Behind these the windows were sealed shut.

He left the apartment, closing the door quietly behind him, and waited for Turnow or Mrs. Boychuck to appear. When the corridor stayed empty, he let himself into the apartment opposite, once more with as little sound as possible. Salter had already checked it out, according to Turnow. Pickett thought he knew why. If it was known to be empty, and was as easy to get into from outside as Linda Thomas's apartment, it made a useful place for a rapist to wait and listen.

This apartment was decorated with more panache than that of Linda Thomas. There was a huge blowup of Superman; several large photographs of people caught unawares, subtitled with the names of the seven deadly sins; and, hanging alone in the middle of one wall, a fantastic stuffed cloth figure about three feet long of a sprite with green hair and with one leg ending in a flower instead of a foot. A huge sign hung over the entrance to the living room. It was in two parts on either side of a wooden cherub perched above the door. NOSMO was on one side, KING on the other. Pickett smiled, wondering how many people in Toronto had heard of the entertainer of that name he used to listen to on the BBC when he was stationed in England during the war.

He checked that the window was fastened and the dust undisturbed around the catches. Before he left he looked through the peephole into the corridor, then stood behind the front door and waited. He was rewarded in a few minutes with the sound of Turnow's voice.

"He's not out yet," Turnow said quietly but clearly from along the corridor.

"Come away," Mrs. Turnow said, also quietly but just as clearly. "Leave it. Keep your nose clean. This is a good job for us."

A door closed along the corridor.

Pickett came out and closed the door loudly behind him, but no head popped out from the janitor's apartment. His last stop was at Mrs. Boychuck's. He wanted to know if she had some gossip to offer. She was more than willing to share what she had. Pickett accepted the offer of a cup of coffee and listened to her account of life next door.

"She had a lot of callers," Mrs. Boychuck began. "She would, wouldn't she, doing what she did?" She was a little woman in her seventies who nodded continuously as she talked, though not, as far as Pickett could tell, from any disease.

"What was that?"

"She was some type of counselor, wasn't she? Psychological? And she did typing, too. I heard her typing a lot."

"What did she tell you she did?"

"Therapist, she called herself. That right?"

Pickett settled himself into his chair, not questioning anybody, his body said. Just having a nice chat. "Could you hear her with her clients?"

"Oh, sure. Not the words, but you could hear them talking."

"Just talking?" Pickett sipped his coffee and winked.

"Yes. Not like the Hungarian lady who was there before. Zsa Zsa, we called her. What a performance her and her boyfriend used to put on! And then when you met them coming out of the apartment, he'd lift his hat. Very good manners, he had. Both of them were very polite, but when they were inside with the door closed they made a terrible racket. Not fighting, you know, enjoying themselves."

"Did you know Miss Thomas well?"

"Just a little bit. She seemed like a very nice lady. Offered to get my groceries once or twice when it was cold, but I like to go out. I'm on my own now and my daughter is in Windsor and my son's so busy that shopping is my only chance to get out and see people.''

''Did you hear anything that afternoon? Did she have a lot of visitors? More than one?'' He held his cup out for more coffee.

''No, I heard her in there with someone, then I heard her say good-bye, calling down the hall. You can't help hearing in these apartments.'' She put her tongue in her cheek. I'm not a snoop, the gesture said, but I'm not going to pass up a bit of entertainment.

''Did you hear the door close and open again?''

''No. I heard someone leave about four o'clock and her saying good-bye and something about a shower. Nothing after that. I was watching television, but I think I would have heard anyone else.''

''Did you ever see any of the people who came to her apartment?''

''A few, I did. Yes. One or two.''

''If I brought you some pictures, could you tell me if anyone looks familiar?''

''I could try, couldn't I?''

Pickett walked to the window and looked out over the parking lot. ''Did you see anyone hanging around the parking lot that day?''

''Not that afternoon, no. And I would've. I've got my chair so that I can look out when I'm watching television. I like to see the sky.''

''Do you know her other neighbor? The woman across the hall?''

"Oh, yes, very well. I look after her herbs when she's away."

"You check it every day?"

"Not every day. I usually look in when I come back from church on Sundays, and then once more during the week."

"Did you go in last Sunday?"

"Yes, just in and out. I was waiting for my son to pick me up. He gets short-tempered if I don't answer the buzzer right away."

A good witness, Pickett thought. She's enjoying the excitement, but she's not going to pretend to anything, just to sound important. "I'll come back," he said, standing up. He gave her his card and reeled off the usual little speech about getting in touch with him if she thought of anything that might help.

When he went out into the corridor, Turnow was standing in his doorway, waiting for him.

"I'll be right with you," Pickett said, walking past him and letting himself into the dead woman's apartment, shutting the door behind him. In the bathroom he closed the door and pulled the shower curtain halfway along, then turned the shower on full. The shower head was so badly corroded that only about a third of the holes let water through, and the angle of the jets varied from straight down to nearly sideways. One of the holes had been so enlarged by rust that it created a thin jet of water with the power of a drill. He turned off the shower and dried himself with a handkerchief, then returned to Mrs. Boychuck's apartment, passing a wondering Turnow in the corridor.

"Tell me again about the person you heard leaving," he asked her. "What did she say to him about a shower?"

"I didn't hear it all. Just sort of 'bye' and then something, something, something 'a shower.' It sounded to me like she was telling him she was going to have a shower."

"A man?"

"I'm sure it was a he. Very firm steps, you know."

"And you're sure she said 'good-bye'?"

"Oh, I think so. She sort of called after him, the way you do when you're waving."

"And he called back what?"

"I couldn't hear. He said something, but he was too far away."

"Fine. Thanks." Pickett let himself out into the corridor. Turnow was still standing in his doorway, waiting for him.

"Finished with the keys? Mrs. Boychuck hear anything?"

Pickett dropped the keys into Turnow's hand, considering the question. Turnow lied so much he was easy to spot when he did it. "She heard Linda Thomas say something about a shower," he said. "She ever complain to you about it? Ask you to fix it?"

"Shower?" Turnow looked genuinely and honestly puzzled. "I didn't know she had any problem."

Satisfied, Pickett turned away and was called back by Mrs. Turnow's voice. "Ask him in, Larry. I want to tell him."

Turnow looked at Pickett and jerked his head in the direction of his wife's voice, looking angry. Pickett walked into the living room, where Mrs. Turnow was sitting, smoking. She waited for the two men to sit down, then said, "I've something to say that I've already told the other policeman."

Turnow immediately stood up, walked over to the window, and arranged himself dramatically, one hand on the window frame the other in his pocket, his back turned to the room. "It's just you speculating," he said over his shoulder. "I've told you, there's no reason to talk about her like that. She was a therapist."

"Therapist," the woman said contemptuously.

"Like what?" Pickett asked.

"She was running a parlor."

Pickett contrived to look blank.

"Sex," she said.

"You know that?"

"She gave massage. When a woman gives a man massage, that's what it is."

"Were all her customers men?"

"All the ones I saw."

"She had women, too," Turnow said over his shoulder. "That make her a dike? Knock it off, Bonnie. You don't know anything about it. She was just doing typing and therapy."

"Do typists give their customers lovey-dovey kisses when they leave?"

"You saw her kissing one of her clients?" Pickett asked.

"Yes, I did. One Friday afternoon. Well, I heard them. I was just closing my door and I heard them in the hall. In her doorway. I'd phoned her earlier to see if I could look at a television set she was wanting to sell. She said she had a client coming that afternoon. Client." The woman lit a cigarette, and moved an ashtray an eighth of an inch closer to her. "She was a prostitute."

A prostitute who kissed the clients good-bye? Pickett wondered. An amateur, then. In a small way of business, too. "We've still got to find out who killed her," he said.

"That's why I'm telling you, not to blacken her. You'll have to be very lucky, won't you? She could've had dozens of clients, so-called, and you'll never find out who they are. You won't know their names."

Pickett said, "You don't agree with your wife, Mr. Turnow?"

"I've got no reason to, have I? She was just a tenant as far as I was concerned. Easier than most."

"You knew what your wife thought?"

"Yes, and I told her she was wrong." He turned around to face them. "She sure as hell didn't roll over for me, I'll tell you." He was talking to both of them.

No one spoke for a few moments. Then the woman said, "It wasn't you I was worried about, Larry. It was the good name of the building."

Pickett decided he had been told what the woman had to say and prepared to go. Then he thought of something: "Have there been any callers since she was killed?"

"No one in person. Her brother phoned from somewhere in the States, saying he'd let me know what we should do about her stuff."

"If there are any inquiries, take their name and address and tell them to get in touch with me. And *you* get in touch, too. Okay?" He moved toward the door. "If her brother calls again tell him we're not ready to release anything yet. That apartment is sealed. I don't want anyone in there."

"What about an emergency, if a pipe bursts or something?" Turnow's face took on a slightly pious, responsible air.

"Dial 911. When the squad car comes, tell them why you have to go in, and they'll go in with you. Many thanks." He made a point of shaking hands with them both.

Pickett walked around the building, trying to estimate how long a stranger would have to spend climbing in the balcony window of the apartment. About two minutes, he thought, and as long as he adopted a rudimentary disguise—a carpenter's apron would do—no one would take any notice.

Before he reported back to Salter, he bought a sandwich at a fast-food outlet and ate it in his car while he wrote up his notes. It took him twenty minutes, but he wanted to be ready for Salter when he walked in the door.

FOUR

"HERE'S HER DIARY," Salter said. "She had two appointments that day. The first was with an architect named Gormley—Henry Gormley. He'd been there before, several times. The second one, about the time she was killed, was just marked 'Abe.'"

"Can I see?" Pickett held out his hand for the book. He flicked through the early pages. "Abe'd been there before, too. Could he be a friend? There's no phone number."

"There are a couple more like that, though. No phone numbers. Either she knew them well, or they did the phoning every time."

"How many have we identified?"

"Four, apart from the ones with just first names. All of them have alibis, if we're even thinking like that."

"Including the one who's making a stink? The civil servant?"

"Oh, yes. The detectives who questioned him thought they would be smart. They tried pointing out that if she *was* a hooker then it would look pretty funny when his name cropped up. He hit the roof and got them taken off the case. He's got important friends, this one."

"Do I have to worry about that?" Pickett watched Salter carefully.

Salter, in turn, looked for several seconds at Pickett. "I'd like to say no, but I don't know you well enough. Will you get me into trouble? We're all being very cagey at the moment."

"I won't threaten him, but I'll treat him like a suspect. Which he is."

"Do what you have to do, but do it strictly by the rules. If he makes a run for it, aim for his feet."

Pickett smiled.

Salter continued. "If I plan to suspend you, I'll let you know so you can retire first."

"Fair enough." Pickett smiled again. "What about this TV guy? You ever see him?"

"No, but everyone else has. He's a household word, they tell me. He's completely cooperative."

"And then there's this guy Abe."

"And then there's Abe. We don't have a thing on him."

Pickett thumbed through his notes. "If she was putting out for her clients, this deputy minister is being pretty cool. He's taking a chance we won't find someone who paid her for sex."

"What do you think?"

"I'll have to talk to him first. Unless he's a gambler, I'd say his reaction makes it unlikely. Did he want to be left out of the inquiry?"

"He just doesn't want the world to know he went to a therapist, and he doesn't see why they should. He's shy, I guess. Would you be?"

"I might, in his position. People might think I was cracking up."

"What did you think of her apartment?"

"It didn't look like any hooker's place I've ever seen. No fancy underwear, stuff like that."

"She'd had sex that afternoon."

"So she wasn't killed by a frustrated client. So, probably, apart from the janitor's wife and my own dirty mind, she was a straight-up therapist and typist."

"Who got strangled. What did you make of the janitor?"

"I'll tell you what I made of him. There's an old lady I know, a widow, lives in an apartment near Eglinton and Yonge. She belonged to my wife's church, and my wife used to make sure she was okay, because she didn't have any family. This old lady calls me once in a while if she wants something fixed, a picture hung or a washer on a tap, anything small like that. The reason she calls me is she's got a janitor like this guy. Arrogant, lazy bastard who won't do nothing. Nothing. See, the block was fine when she moved in, they had a nice husband-and-wife couple looking after it. But about three years ago the owners sold out to some rich sonofabitch who saw a chance to make a lot more money. Right away the building started to fall apart. He stopped cleaning the place, closed up the

garbage chutes so they had to take their garbage outside, and tried to jack up all the rents on the grounds
he had this big mortgage he had to take out to buy the
block. They had to form a tenants' association and
fight him in court. He was even subdividing the
apartments to get twice the rent. What he wanted was
to get this old lady and all the other old ladies out of
there so he could charge more. Anyway, the janitor
was fired and since then this bastard has put in four or
five janitors, each one worse than the last. They're *his*
janitors, see, and the bastard *wants* them to be lousy.
I doubt if he pays them. If the old ladies complained,
the owner told them to move. But they've stuck it out
and they go to court once a month and refuse to pay
their rent until he cleans the place up, and they look to
be winning. But it's a hell of a way to spend your old
age, trying to keep your apartment building nice. This
guy nails notices to their doors, ordering them out.
Those fake bailiff's notices.''

"Doesn't the city help?''

"Oh, sure. They send in building inspectors who
serve him with notices, ordering him to turn on the
heat. This guy is breaking every bylaw. But you have
to take him to court each time and he doesn't care. He
knows every trick in the book, especially about post-
poning court hearings. I even called the alderman.
She's got a reputation for being on the side of the
people. She told me to get the old lady out of there
because the landlord will win in the end. How's that
for an answer? Anyway, this janitor is on that wave-

length. Doing the minimum, not worried about his job. Screw the tenants; they're a dime a dozen. Worry about the guy who hires you. Turnow and his wife get a little worried when we come around in case they're breaking some law on the landlord's behalf. Stupid, ignorant, and bone-fucking-idle, that's Turnow."

Salter seemed to be listening, but when Pickett stopped he went back to his opening remarks. "How long have you been married?" he asked.

"My wife died a little while ago. We'd been married for forty years." Pickett's face showed his puzzlement.

"Was it hard, when you were in Homicide? Did your wife mind being married to a cop?"

"Why? Your wife complaining?" Pickett grinned. "It was hard, sure. I saw a lot of marriages go on the rocks. But I was lucky, I guess. My wife didn't take it personally when I didn't come home until midnight or not at all. She had her own thing. She was a dressmaker, and she kept it up after we got married. Got a few pins in the meatloaf sometimes, but what the hell. And she didn't drink, like some of them do." He waited to see if there was anything more, but the chat seemed to be over. He slipped his notebook into his pocket. "I'll go talk to these people," he said.

HE HAD NO TROUBLE getting to see Fred Doughty; the TV host was eager to make time for him, and the two men arranged to meet at his town house on McGill Street at noon the next day.

Doughty's house was one of several on the street that had been given violent and expensive surgery to transform them from aging working-class cottages to desirable bijou residences "just steps from downtown." Doughty's house had been facelifted rather then renovated; it looked as it must have done when it was first built, eighty or ninety years before, except for the sky-blue front door. The front of the house had had its parts capped, as if every brick had been extracted and replaced by an identical but brand-new brick, and the same thing had happened to the windows and the new/antique drainpipe. Pickett half expected to see authentic vegetables growing in the front garden, but here the owner had sacrificed art for the sake of somewhere to park his car.

Doughty met him at the door of the house and took him up to the living room, or space, or area, which took up most of the second floor. Pickett had an impression of a lot of sofas, some thousands of books, and half a wall of electronic equipment. "Will you have a beer?" Doughty asked. "I've been waiting to have my one and only nooner."

Pickett unbuttoned his jacket and settled himself comfortably in an armchair that seemed made for a giant. "Sure."

The host disappeared into the kitchen and returned with two cans of beer. "It's okay to drink on duty?" he asked.

"It depends." Pickett took a sip of his beer. "I'm just here to talk to you about Miss Thomas. It's lunchtime. I don't want to upset your routine. Besides, we could've met in a bar. Why? You going to report me?" Pickett worked to get Doughty in focus. The khaki pants, the gray sweatshirt with RYERSON over the heart, the sneakers, the tightly cut hair—they belonged to no type Pickett was familiar with. By his face, the man was in his midforties, but he seemed as physically trim as his own hair. He was extremely unpretty; apart from his nose, which was a neat, finely pointed triangle, the rest of his face was knobby and battered, as if he had spent half his life in the stocks, having turnips thrown at him. He looked like a pug with a heart of gold and very good taste.

Doughty laughed. "No way. How do we start? You have some questions?"

He moved over to the wall and pressed some buttons.

"What's this?" Pickett asked. "What are you doing?"

"Do you mind if I tape this? I'd like a record."

"What for? You can't use it. I should be taping *you* down at headquarters."

"I'd still want my own record. I'll give you a copy of this tape."

"What do you want a record *for?*"

"Call it second nature. The business I'm in. I'd like to have a tape for my files."

Pickett thought, Why not? What do I care? Then a possibility occurred to him. "You don't mean videotape?" He didn't care much if Salter took him off the ob, but he didn't want to wind up on television, ooking like a horse's ass.

Doughty laughed. "Cross my heart. No *Candid Camera*. Just sound. Okay?"

Pickett shrugged and Doughty pressed another button. Ten thousand monkeys chattered, then the ape began slowly to roll forward.

"What do you want to know?" Doughty asked. "I already told your people everything I know."

Pickett nodded. "It's easier for me if I hear you tell t. First of all, you were a regular client of hers. Right?"

"I had an appointment every two weeks, usually on Wednesday afternoons."

"How did you get on to her?"

"She was recommended. Word of mouth, call it. A lady I know."

"Did you know any of her other clients?"

"None. I never passed anyone in the hall or surprised anyone coming out. For all I knew I was her only client." Doughty leaned forward. "Why aren't you taking notes?"

Pickett considered the question and where it might be coming from. "This is old ground. The other two took notes. They're in the file."

"You usually take notes, though."

"Always. Mostly one asks the questions and the other takes it down. We usually work in pairs."

"Then you both sign the notes?"

What was Doughty on about? Was he being tricky? "You want me to take notes?"

"No, no. I'll give you a copy of the tape."

"So I don't need to write it down. Now, can we get on? Where were you when she was killed?"

"I was shopping."

"What did you buy?"

"Nothing. I was just window-shopping. All afternoon."

Now for the sensitive bit: "What do you know about Linda Thomas?"

Simultaneously Doughty asked, "How will you check up on my alibi?"

"What?"

"My alibi. How will you check up on it?"

Pickett, waiting for an answer to his question, wondered what Doughty was talking about. "Alibi?"

"Yes. I can't prove I was shopping."

"You mean you weren't?"

"No, I mean, how will you prove it, or not?"

"I'll take your word for it. If we don't find the guy who killed her soon, I might come back to it." He thought of something. "Your name Abe?"

"Abe?" Now Doughty looked baffled.

"Yeah. You call yourself Abe? To your girlfriends?"

"I don't understand. My name's Fred."

"There you are, then. I'm not looking for a Fred. Let's get back to what you knew about Linda

Thomas." Pickett felt he was holding his own in whatever was going on.

"You asked me where I was when Linda was killed."

"That's routine. You said 'shopping,' right. That's the answer."

"But I could be lying."

What was this tit on about? "You want to know how I eliminate you?"

"That's it. How do you eliminate me?"

"First of all, I have to suspect you, which I don't. Then I follow up with some more questions. What's this all about? I'll investigate you if you like, but I thought you wanted us to be discreet, you being famous and all. Okay, try this: Did you go into any stores?"

"One or two."

"Which ones?"

Doughty named three.

"Did they recognize you?"

"Clever. If I say 'No,' so much for my image. If I say 'Yes,' then you can check up on me."

"That's right. See, if you weren't famous, I'd have more of a problem. I'll check up on these when I'm in the area."

Doughty grinned and blushed slightly. "If you do check up, you'll find I wasn't there."

"Then where were you?"

"Over at Ryerson. I was talking to my son's class. I got there around two-thirty and they wouldn't let me go until five. My son is taking a degree there."

"So what's all this crap about shopping?"

"Do you mind if I tell you later? I'd like our conversations to be as unaffected as possible."

Unaffected? "Don't forget, though, will you? You've got me all excited now. Could we get back to Miss Thomas? Without any more screwing around? What do you know about her?"

"Not much. A nice girl. Good at massage. Believed in what she was doing, more than I did. I just wanted someone to untwist me, but she believed in massage as one of the doors to psychic health. She was fairly new to it, and she had been told to be very careful about who she took on. You had to be recommended."

"Who recommended you? A lady, you say. Who?"

"Let's call her a lady of my choice. Her name is Julie Sands. She's a writer-producer for the CBC."

Pickett thought about his next question. Doughty was on the edge of the couch, eager, inviting questions. Pickett plunged in, headfirst. "If you were recommended by a lady, then this is probably unnecessary, but, you know, massage has gotten a funny name. Let's put it this way: How much did she charge?"

Doughty closed his eyes and moved his head firmly left to right and back again. "Not a chance. Have you ever had a massage?"

Pickett shook his head.

"You should try it. Oh, it might cross your mind the first time, but she was absolutely impeccable. The thing is, it *is* very intimate, very comforting, and she was attractive enough, so I guess it could happen that someone might think she was available. But I'm certain that if anyone tried anything, *anything*, that would be the last time. She was a therapist."

"Did she talk to you while she was giving massage?"

"Not a lot. The idea is to empty your mind."

"She never gave you any idea who her other clients were? You know, barbers, they're always telling you about their other customers."

"She never did."

Pickett sipped the last of his beer. He had nothing more to ask, but he felt in Doughty a desire to talk.

"That it?" Doughty asked.

"Yes, thanks. You've been very helpful." Pickett made motions of buttoning his jacket and looking at his watch.

"Would you mind answering a few questions for me before you go?"

"This about your alibi?"

"Sort of. First of all, when you found the body, you called in the experts, the police doctor, people like that?"

Pickett looked at the tape deck. "You going to put this on TV?"

"No, don't worry about that. This is just personal."

"You keep a diary on tape?"

"Hey," Doughty grinned. "That's an idea. Maybe I'll try that. No, I'm thinking of something else. A story. A novel."

"A whodunit?"

"No, no, a real novel. About the interpenetrating lives of a number of people whose relationships are concretized, changed, and revealed by the sudden death of one of them. I want to use the police inquiry as a device. As they answer the police questions they begin to see themselves and their relationships differently than they did before. The truth, though, won't come out until the very end, when the murderer is revealed and the reader realizes that he has a way of testing the truth of everything he has so far heard, but it won't be the physical truth so much as the psychological truth that will be recalled, not what the characters did, but why they acted the way they did."

"Motive? Something like that?" Without waiting for a reply, Pickett went on. "What do you want me to tell you?"

Doughty hunched himself forward, his wrists on his knees. "I'd like to follow this case so that I understand procedure, police procedure. I need the technical information."

"I don't see how I can help, Mr. Doughty. You want me to phone you every day? Tell you what the people said? Stuff like that? I couldn't do that. They'd have my ass."

"I'm not interested in this case. Don't tell me anything confidential, just how you are going about the job. Nothing I couldn't find out from any Metro detective on a homicide case."

"Nothing about this case?"

"Nothing you wouldn't tell a reporter."

The tape clicked to a stop and Doughty jumped up to put on a fresh reel.

"You want to know how we do our job?"

"That's it. I thought it would be easier to follow this case."

"You could go down to headquarters. Or to Homicide. They'd probably help you out." Pickett dodged a clear answer. He would have to okay it with Salter. But he was intrigued, flattered. Why say no so long as he stuck to public information? Nevertheless, he waited for Doughty's response, waited to see if there were problems.

"As you say, I'm too well known." A statement of fact, made without vanity.

Not to me, Pickett thought. "Not to me," he said.

"*Touché,* but if I went down to your headquarters, we couldn't have a straight conversation. My image *would* get in the way."

The only question that remained was whether Pickett wanted to be bothered. One conversation wouldn't be enough; Doughty would probably bug him all the time he was writing his book. Would he mind that? He decided if he did that he could cut him off then. Right now he saw no reason to back off. "Okay," he said. "You want it from the beginning?"

Doughty looked at his watch. "Let's have a sandwich," he said. "Roast beef okay? I've got ham or smoked turkey as well."

"Beef will be fine."

Doughty had the lunch ready in seconds and put on some water to boil for coffee. He put a sandwich in front of Pickett and leaned back with his own sandwich, ready to receive. Then for half an hour, while Doughty tiptoed around, changing tapes, refilling coffee cups, very occasionally asking a question, Pickett explained how they went about investigating a homicide. "So there it is," he concluded. "Now I have to interview everyone connected with the case, find out who her friends were, talk to them."

"You know who was with her that afternoon?"

"We're just talking generally, you said."

"Sorry, but it could have been someone in the apartment block couldn't it? How do you cover that?"

"We send a detective door-to-door. Me, in this case."

"What about an outsider, someone walking in off the street?"

"That's the hardest. Someone totally unconnected with her got into the apartment thinking it was empty, then killed her." He waited for Doughty to respond. "Anything else?"

Doughty swung back to him. "This is terrific," he said. "Terrific. Can I follow it up? Call you?"

"Sure. What for?"

"Just for details. Make sure I get things accurate, you know? Like how much policemen earn, that kind of thing."

"Sure. Here's a card. Call me anytime you like. Leave a message if I'm not there. Maybe not, if you're that famous. Here." He took the card back and wrote a number on it. "Call me at home. So why did you tell me you were shopping in Yorkville?"

"I thought it would be interesting to see how you confirmed it, and what happened when you couldn't. I would have told you eventually, of course."

"After you'd had us pissing around for a week. Don't play any more games like that. Ask me what you want to know."

"Sorry. It seemed like a real opportunity. I won't bother you unless I'm really stuck. I would guess policemen's wives don't like them being bothered when they're off duty?"

"My wife died a few years ago. I've got an answering machine, so leave a message and I'll call you back."

The front door opened and a tall youth with a mess of black hair and wearing an old hotel doorman's overcoat that reached to his ankles came in. "Sorry," he said when he saw Pickett. "I won't get in the way. I just came in for a quick protein fix." He stood waiting to be dismissed, and Doughty introduced him to

Pickett. "How do you do, sir," the boy said, shaking hands.

"Tim is in Radio and Television Arts at Ryerson," Doughty said. "It's only five minutes away, so he saves money on subway fares and meals by living here."

"I compensate for the disadvantage of having a famous father by living off him. Now, if Sergeant Pickett will excuse me, I'll just see what there is to eat around here." He moved past them, bowing, into the kitchen.

"His mother got married again," Doughty said. "So he moved in with me last fall. It's handy for his classes."

Pickett stood up. "I don't think I'll have to bother you again," he said. "But feel free when you're writing your book."

"Thanks." Doughty ushered Pickett through the door.

THE INTERVIEW with the deputy minister was much less congenial. Pickett gave his name to the receptionist in Queen's Park at five minutes before the appointed time and was asked to take a seat far enough away from the desk so he could not hear the conversation as she announced him on the telephone. He leafed through a magazine lying on the low table in front of the visitors' couch. It was a house organ, full of stories and pictures about the employees of the Ontario government. One of the pictures was of a dinner given in honor of a retiring civil servant. The caption identified the two central figures in the picture as the deputy minister and his wife. Pickett waited for the receptionist to turn her head and slipped the magazine into his raincoat pocket. Ten minutes later he was directed to an office along a corridor, where he introduced himself to an executive assistant who asked him to take another seat, but this time Pickett stayed on his feet, affecting to look at pictures on the walls of the reception room. Five minutes elapsed before he was told to go in.

The deputy minister leaned back in his chair to watch the sergeant enter. He let a few seconds pass, then motioned to a chair close to the front of his desk. Pickett moved the chair back a couple of feet and angled it sideways to the desk. He took off his coat, folded it into a neat pile on the floor by his chair, and sat down.

The deputy minister stayed leaning back in his chair. "I can give you five minutes," he said.

Pickett nodded and thumbed slowly through his notebook. "Mr. Curry? Mr. Nicholas Curry?" He flicked his thumb to turn back a page, and looked up.

"Who did you expect to find behind this desk? Mickey Mouse?"

"I'm just making sure. I didn't know but what there mightn't be another office through there." He pointed to the door in the corner behind Curry. "And you were mebbe your assistant."

"That's the can."

"Got your own, eh?" Pickett made a face to show he was impressed. "Handy if you get caught short. Now, sir, I have to ask you some questions about the death of Linda Thomas."

The front legs of Curry's chair came crashing down as he shot forward and planted his wrists on the desk. "I've already answered enough questions about that. Two of your pals have been in already."

"I know. I've read their notes. But, see, the case has come to me now, and I have to go over it all again. Ten minutes should do it."

Curry looked at him with contempt, which was how Pickett wanted him, contemptuous and off his guard. He was, Pickett guessed, at least six feet tall. He looked thin only because of his height. Wavy hair; a bony, handsome face; and a trick of pulling his lips wide when he spoke, hissing the major nouns with disgust. He dressed like an English financier: gray suit of a very thin material, gold cuff links, a striped shirt. The only flaw in his appearance came from the coarseness of his skin, which looked as though it had spent too long exposed to bad weather. His face was an archipelago of red blotches, and even his hands, though beautifully manicured, had the same raw look, as if they had been recently boiled.

"Let me tell you two things," Curry said. "One: I know nothing about Miss Thomas's death. I last visited her establishment more than three weeks ago. I had no intention of returning after that visit, nor did I. On the afternoon she died, I was on a train coming from Ottawa. My wife met me at the station. The second thing is that I can make things happen to any policeman who tries to get smart. A word, Sergeant"—he emphasized the title, pulling his lips wide—"that's all it would take from me."

"To do what?" Pickett tried to look wary and puzzled.

"To send you packing."

So far, Pickett considered that he had been a model of politeness—servile, almost—but he was getting bored with it, and if Curry was going to keep this up he would have to consider telling the deputy minister to go fuck himself, and go home and get the bag of gold. "I'll go now if you like," he offered. "Someone else would be along, though. I'm here because of you. You had one of your words, and the case got shifted to Special Affairs."

Curry nodded, unsurprised, pleased.

"We're trained to be very discreet. Now, can I ask you some questions?"

Curry looked at his watch. "You have three minutes."

Pickett stood up. "I'll come back tomorrow, shall I?"

"No, get on with it."

Pickett then confirmed what he already knew, that Curry claimed to have taken the Ottawa train on Thursday, to have spent the morning on government business and returned the next afternoon on the train, being met by his wife at the station. It was a trip he took regularly.

"Always...by...train." Pickett wrote it down, slowly.

"I dislike planes."

This out of the way, Pickett asked him what he knew about Linda Thomas.

"Nothing. Nothing at all. I had several treatments from her and decided not to continue."

"Why, sir? Why was that?"

"She wasn't much good."

Pickett shook his head, sympathetically. "How did you get on to her?"

"She was recommended by a friend."

"Did you know any of her other customers?"

"She never mentioned her other clients to me, or me to them, I hope."

"We got your name from her appointment book," Pickett reassured him.

"So I understand. Now, if you're satisfied, I don't want my name to appear anywhere else. Is that clear? Shall I tell you why? If the word gets out around here that I went to a psychotherapist, they will assume I have psychological problems, and if they hear the word 'massage' they will assume she was a whore. Neither one is true. As you must have established, she was a professional therapist, even if she was not a very good one. But my minister is from Windsor, and for him massage means parlors, and he would worry about that. Now do you understand?"

"We understand, sir," Pickett said. "Don't worry about us. No need for anyone to know what you do. Except your wife, of course."

"Why my wife? Why does she have to be involved?"

"Doesn't she know you went to a therapist?" Before Curry could reply to this ingenuous-sounding query, Pickett continued, "'Cause I'll have to confirm that she met the train, see. Just to tick you off my list."

Curry looked at the policeman for a long time, while Pickett rearranged the rubber band that kept his place in his notebook, waiting for Curry to see his problem.

Finally Curry said, "We'll be home at six tonight, sharp." He gave Pickett an address in Wychwood Park. "Let me explain how to get there."

"I know how to get to Wychwood Park. I live right by."

"You live there?" Curry spoke quietly, but he underlined every word in disbelief.

"Just across the streetcar tracks." Pickett looked at his watch. "My time must be up." He picked up his coat.

"Once more then, Sergeant, you screw this up and get my name in the press, or even whispered around here, and you are in deep shit."

He's very worried, thought Pickett, and the reflection saved him from telling Curry where he could stuff it. "See you at six," he said. "Sharp."

FIVE

THERE WERE TWO HOURS to spare before he had to be at Curry's house, and Pickett decided to spend the time at home. His tenant had asked him that morning to look at the upstairs toilet, which did not seem to be working properly. Pickett enjoyed being a landlord. Most of his tenants so far had been couples, married and unmarried, who stayed about a year, or single girls, who tended to stay six months. Pickett had been lucky with all of them. He had no rules, and no one had abused the lack of them. If the girls had overnight visitors, they came and went discreetly enough (there was no separate entrance), and Pickett had made his own bedroom in the basement, so small parties on the second floor did not bother him.

He parked in front of the house and let himself through the back door into the kitchen, where Willis, the dog, went mad with joy at seeing him home so early. Willis, a tiny, hairy, grinning creature—a present for his wife in her last illness—was housebroken but otherwise untrainable, and he had to walk her on a leash twice a day, which made him feel foolish at first because it was like walking a flea on a piece of string. But he was used to it now and even enjoyed the mildly absurd figure the two of them made. Besides, the dog was indiscriminately affectionate—a tart, the vet called her—and because of her he was well known in the neighborhood. Everyone wanted to pat her.

The dog followed him up to the second floor, where Pickett fixed the chain inside the toilet tank, then came back down to the kitchen to make himself a cup of tea. He heard the door in the adjoining house open as his neighbor arrived home, and he considered whether this was a good time to ask her what she wanted to do about the mutual fence, which needed repairing. He was on good terms with this neighbor, a librarian in her fifties whose drive he shoveled clear of snow and whose grass he cut when he cut his own, and who, in return, looked after Willis when Pickett was away. Partly because of her, he had begun reading again, for the first time since adolescence. In the beginning he thought he had gotten out of the habit because the books he tried, the current best-selling paperbacks, seemed to be written for someone else. He tried pornography in the form of novels written about life in Hollywood but found himself unengaged after three or four hundred pages. He tried the classics, but read the whole of only one Dickens novel, *Our Mutual Friend,* because he had liked the television version. He tried Hardy, who turned out to be ashes all the way, and he tried Trollope, again because of the television series, but the books were a disappointment after the television version of them. And then, at the suggestion of his neighbor, he tried Arnold Bennett and found himself home at last, in an area unknown to him before, the English popular novelists of the 1920s and 1930s. He read his way through Bennett, moved on to J. B. Priestley, quite liked Galsworthy, found Somerset Maugham talked too much, and was currently rereading Bennett's *Buried Alive*.

He looked at the clock on the stove; it was five-twenty. He decided to postpone discussion of the fence until the weekend. It was time to get back to work. He left the house feeling more strongly than ever that his work was interfering with his life at home.

WYCHWOOD PARK is a toy village carved out of the middle of Toronto, like a diplomatic enclave in a Far Eastern Capital. It was created to give a few dozen citizens a sense of exclusivity, and it has survived all the attempts of left-wing politicians to integrate it into its surroundings. The road in is private and unwelcoming, but once inside, all is pastoral and benign. A sense of things rural is created by the many trees, by the gravel roads, and by the swan on the little pond. It is easy here to shut out the knowledge of the streetcar barns a hundred yards away on the other side of the trees, and the teeming multicultural world of working-class Toronto that surrounds the village. It is a Dingley Dell in aspic, a Forest of Arden where a few fortunate citizens can go into exile after a hard day at the office.

Pickett had walked Willis here once or twice and had no trouble finding Curry's house. It was typical of the enclave, a large manor that mixed leaded windows and aluminum siding, as though created out of several different kits. Pickett noted a two-car garage that held only a boxy, four-wheel-drive vehicle and drove by, parking around the bend in the road so that he could watch, more or less out of sight, Curry arrive. He appeared at a quarter to six and Pickett waited fourteen minutes, then drove up to the front door.

Curry opened the door and stood back for him to enter. "Let's get this over with," he said, and led the way into the living room. For the first time, Pickett envied Curry, for it was a handsome room, with polished plank flooring, a fieldstone fireplace, and some superb old furniture. Pickett had begun to find out a bit about antique furniture, thinking he might try his hand at restoring, and even with the little he knew, he could appreciate the amount and quality of the mahogany, rosewood, and oak that Curry had evidently collected.

Mrs. Curry was waiting, her arms crossed, her back to the fire. Curry introduced Pickett and stood to one side as a signal to the sergeant to proceed. No one sat down.

Curry's wife was almost as tall as he was, a thin woman who had retained the yellow curls of her youth into middle-aged girlishness. Her face, too, though somewhat lined, still had the high coloring that must once have made her doll-like. "You want to know about my husband and this therapist he goes to?" Her voice was light and slightly cracked.

Pickett said nothing.

"I knew all about her. He wanted me to try her, but I'm not keen on that kind of thing. It seems to do him good, though. He needs help relaxing."

It was brightly said, but she was too noisy. There was a faint glaze in the woman's manner, as if she were keeping up her end of the conversation during intermission at a theater. She looked around Pickett rather than at him.

"All that really matters is that I account for your husband on the day she was killed."

"You can do that. He was in Ottawa, and I met him off the afternoon train, as usual. I always pick him up when he returns from Ottawa."

"All right, Sergeant? Can we end this now?" Curry cut in.

"I guess so." Pickett knew that he couldn't get past the wife's story, the possibility that she was lying, without some luck. It was going to be necessary to separate these two, find some inconsistency (Did she find a parking space? Did she wait with her engine running, double-parked?). Later, perhaps when he found a reason. Curry would not stand still for much more now. Thus far his status protected him.

Then the problem was removed. "Ah, I see," Curry said. "The sergeant thinks you may be lying, darling."

Mrs. Curry looked from one to the other. "Of course I'm not lying. Ask Dora, my neighbor. She came down with me so she could sit in the car while I ran into the station and found him. We often chauffeur each other in tricky situations. Shall I call her for you?''

''No need.''

''Good.'' Curry flicked the policeman firmly off his cuff and looked at his watch. ''Darling, we have to leave in half an hour. I'd better change.'' He walked past Pickett and up the stairs, leaving his wife to show the policeman to the door.

SIX

HE BEGAN TO LAY OUT the case on a sheet of paper to prepare a preliminary report for Salter. Something had been done even if there was nothing accomplished, and he had a mystery to unpick as well as a lot of routine work to do. Organizing the story under a number of headings made him feel systematic at least, and ready to talk coherently to the staff inspector. It took him an hour.

Salter was reading a piece of paper when the sergeant walked in, and Pickett took the chair in front of his desk and waited for him to finish. In a few moments Salter grunted, shook his head, then put the note aside. "How long have you been around, Mel?" he asked.

"Forty years, more or less."

"Then you might know the answer to that." Salter nodded toward the piece of paper. "Remind me to show it to you before you go. So. Where are we?"

"I'll start with the stuff I've ticked off."

"Sure. Before you start, we've had a complaint about you. Deputy Minister Nicholas Curry phoned *our* deputy. Said you were clumsy, unintelligent, insensitive, and he's deeply concerned for his privacy if you stay on the case."

Pickett froze at the opening words, then he wanted to laugh because Salter's attitude was perfectly clear: The "we" who had received the complaint included Pickett. Salter was neither admonishing him nor passing on the complaint, merely sharing it with him.

"He only gave me five minutes. I didn't have time to kiss his ass."

"What's the guy like?"

"He's a prick. Sir."

"I know that, but what happened when you saw him?"

Pickett told the story of Curry, in the office and at home, coloring the account with his own reaction as he grew more comfortable with Salter. "I thought the maid was going to show me the back door," he concluded, adding, "I was surprised. Those guys are usually more subtle about letting you know what hotshots they are."

"He's something, isn't he? But it sounds as though we're finished with him. Right?"

"You think he's finished with us? Me?"

Salter considered the question. "You mean will he keep trying to get you off the case?"

"Yeah."

"Probably. But *my* boss is getting a little bored with him. I was there when he got the call. I heard him tell Curry that the case was in the hands of the Special Affairs Unit, and we would use every discretion consistent with carrying out our duty. In other words, fuck off. How old are you?"

"Sixty-two. Why?"

"Why aren't you retired? It's none of my business, I know."

"That's all right. I could retire tomorrow, and I will, too, if I get any more goddamn sensitive cases. I've just been putting it off."

"Then what?"

"Then I'll be retired. Happily."

"This deputy minister isn't about to frighten you, then, is he?"

"No. Screw him. I'd like to stay on the case."

"Good. Let's hear the rest of the report." He motioned to Pickett's notes. "Besides, you don't look ready to retire yet."

Pickett left his notebook untouched. "I don't know if I'm ready. I live alone. My wife died a few years ago. I've stayed in the house. I've duplexed it—but I don't know. There's other stuff." He wanted to talk to this man, tell him his situation, but not if he was just being polite.

"No kids?"

Pickett shook his head.

"A free man."

"That's right. That's why I've been putting it off." Salter looked genuinely interested, and Pickett continued. "I've been thinking about it. I could live pretty good on my pension." He stopped again.

Salter hitched his chair forward. "I only asked to know if Curry would bother you. What you would put up with to stay on the job."

"I don't give a gopher's fart for Curry. But if he bothers you, take me off the case."

"Oh, no. But you never know how things are going to work out."

Pickett returned to his notebook. "The television announcer also has a solid alibi," he continued. "He was giving a lecture. I'll check the other two in her book just to see what they know about her, but one of them was in New York that weekend and the other one was in the hospital—still is—having his gallbladder out." ·

"All men?"

"All the ones in the book."

They had now cleared the ground. There was only one question left. Salter asked it. "So who was with her that afternoon?"

"The guy who killed her, I would think. All we know is, he's called 'Abe.' They drank some wine, then he killed her. One thing bothers me: Mrs. Boychuck heard someone leaving that afternoon, and she heard Thomas saying something about a shower."

"Let's find Abe. Ask him. Any ideas?"

"Not yet. There's a girlfriend gets back from Florida today, and I'm seeing her tomorrow. I'm hoping she'll be able to help." He picked up his notebook and waited to be dismissed. "Apart from her, I have to put everything I've got through a sieve, find out what these people are lying about."

"Who?"

"All of them. The janitor and his wife, Curry and *his* wife, even the TV guy at first, but then he confessed. As I told you, the janitor is the kind of guy who automatically lies until he's sure there's no way he can be nailed for anything. Same with his wife. Either that or he was goofing off all afternoon and doesn't want anyone to find out he takes the afternoon off as well as the rest of the day."

"What's Curry lying about?"

"I don't know. *She's* lying, for sure, and I think he is, too, but I don't know what about. He can prove he wasn't in Toronto that afternoon."

"And the TV guy?"

"He *told* me he was lying. Wanted to see how I broke it down. Wants to write a novel with a murder investigation in it, so we might get some calls. I told him I'd help him get his facts straight. He's not lying now." Pickett gathered himself, preparing to go.

"Hold on a minute." Salter turned to the note he had been reading when Pickett arrived. "You may have an idea about this other thing. Some kid is bugging us about trying to find a relative of hers. She thinks she is related to someone who was in the Canadian Air Force during the war—this kid's English—someone in the Air Force who joined the Toronto police after the war and may still be around. That's more than forty years ago, so I doubt it. But she thinks someone may remember him."

"What's his name?"

"She doesn't know. Her name is Colwood, Imogen Colwood."

"What kind of relative? Uncle or something? How come she doesn't know his name?"

"I figured that out. She's being a bit coy, but my guess is that she's looking for her grandfather who left her grandmother with a baby back in the war, and this kid is trying to track him down. I don't think the guy would want to know now, would he?"

"Maybe not." Pickett seemed to be barely listening.

"He's probably got his own grandchildren. This kid could be embarrassing. So keep it to yourself, but if a likely guy occurs to you, let me know. It's a bit tricky. She doesn't have much to go on and she isn't talking about a legal claim or anything like that. Just wants to take a look at her grandfather, if he's still around. She may be out of luck."

"If I think of anyone, I'll tell you. I know most of the guys my age who are still around."

"I'll talk to her some more, see what kind of problems she might have for him, if she ever finds him."

"Let it lie," Pickett said suddenly. He got up and moved to the door. "I'd better find this Abe."

HE RETURNED to his own office, needing a quiet, empty space where he could react to the news he had heard, turn his emotions into thoughts, his thoughts perhaps into actions. Somewhere like a park bench. He collected his coat and left the building, turning south, looking for a coffee shop. He found what he wanted, an old diner, empty except for the usual pair of Bell Telephone repairmen, ordered a coffee and doughnut from the counter, and took them to an empty corner booth.

Imogen Colwood. Granddaughter of Olive, Leading Aircraft Woman Colwood of the Women's Auxiliary Air Force, stationed in Bournemouth, England, in 1945, where Aircraftsman First Class Pickett had come at the age of nineteen, fresh from failing his air crew training in Brandon, Manitoba.

Pickett had grown up through the Depression and into the war, the only child of a widow who ran a boarding-house to support her son and herself. It had been a solitary childhood; his mother had worked too hard at providing for her son to have any time or energy left for loving him, and he had grown up chained to her fierce maternity but not warmed by it. There was just enough juice left in him at eighteen to take advantage of the war, to use it as an excuse for leaving the nest. He could have been classified as essential to his mother's support, and she knew that, knew that all he wanted was to get away, but they had not talked about it, and he had left one morning, awkwardly, untrained in affection, with not much more emotional display than would have occurred had he been a longtime boarder in the house.

He failed the air crew course and had to accept reclassification as a clerk, the least glamorous of occupations, but he liked the life, and when he found himself posted to England, he could hardly believe his luck. RCAF Bournemouth, where he worked in the orderly room, gave him access to a world so far removed from the boarding-house in Hamilton that he ascribed all of his new content to being in England. The seafront, though barbed and mined against the enemy across the English Channel, filled him with a delight he had never experienced from the Hamilton waterfront. Behind the town were the villages and farms of a Dorset shrunk back by wartime restrictions on travel into a rural peacefulness that seemed to Pickett idyllic. He loved it all—the countryside, the sea, the teashops, the pubs.

Olive Colwood had been "attached" to his orderly room, and in the absence of a corporal in charge, she was his boss. Pickett had done little enough about girls in Hamilton, but his uniform was shifting him into manhood, and Olive arrived and touched him, shattering the thin bubble he lived in that had kept him from the world of affection.

He took her to the station dances and for walks along the cliffs and for bus rides into the countryside. She went home every weekend she could get a pass, but while she was on the station she was his. He knew himself to be more in love than she was—she always retreated from conversations about the future—but he didn't care, sure he could win her over. And then she became pregnant.

After she told him and explained how it could have happened, they took a bus into Christchurch where they sat in a pub and talked until the last bus brought them back to the barracks and they had worked out a plan. She refused to let him marry her, but he insisted on taking care of her.

A few weeks later, Pickett was called in front of his commanding officer, who presented him with the news that a girl called Olive Colwood had named him as the father of her unborn child and asked for the commanding officer's help in making Pickett accept the responsibility. Would he marry her?

Pickett had already consulted his roommates about his position. They offered, as a matter of course, to sign a statement that they had all slept with her, but that wasn't the kind of help he needed. Everyone agreed that if he was fool enough to admit to being the father, he still didn't have to marry her, which was what Pickett wanted to know.

"She says she wants to marry you," the C.O. said.

"But I'm not willing to marry her. She can have all the money I've got. Five hundred pounds. But I won't marry her." He refused to discuss it further.

This was the fifth paternity case the C.O. had dealt with in a month. "I can't force you, and I don't blame you. But why? Try and keep that thing in your pants until you get home, will you?"

Pickett was put on the first available plane to Gander (though he managed a rendezvous with Olive to say good-bye). Back in Hamilton he met Mary Dempster and two years later married her. He got a job with an insurance agency, but after a year he was sick of insurance, Hamilton, and his wife's relatives, and they moved to Toronto, where, after a false start of another year in an insurance agency, he joined the police.

They had a good marriage, and after Mary died, Pickett's colleagues were right at first to assume that he needed his job to fill his days, but five years later he was content again. Now there was this girl—inquiring after him. He tried to think of the consequences of admitting he was the man she was looking for and felt his mind entangled as if in a thornbush. On the other hand, could he ignore the kid? It's a can of worms, he thought. Leave the lid on for the moment. But something about Salter hinted that it might not be as easy as that; the staff inspector's curiosity was aroused, and Pickett concluded that he should stay away from Salter. The only way to do that was to get off the case, which was too bad because so far Salter had been easy to work with. But most of all, Pickett wanted to be left alone. He bought another cup of coffee and spent some time concocting a plausible story, then returned to Salter's office.

"I'VE BEEN THINKING," Pickett began. "I'm pretty sure we're going to have to talk to that deputy minister again, and there could be others. You need a new guy."

"For what? I thought you liked tangling with him."

"I do. I did. But it doesn't do you no good. He's gonna shout and holler if he sees my face again. I don't give a shit, but it'll hold things up if he can get me shifted off the case halfway."

"I don't think he'll be able to do that."

"Even if he doesn't, maybe it'll soften him up if he thinks he's got me." Pickett tried to look cunning.

"We don't know if you have to talk to him again, yet."

"I've got a feeling we will have to. I told you, I think his wife is lying. Covering him up."

Salter considered this. "Okay. This psychologist is nearly off my back. He's designing his questionnaire. He's paid by the day, so it'll take him a week. I'll look after Curry, then, if necessary."

"That's no good, though, is it? Two of us farting around. You should take over the whole thing. Send me back to Bail and Parole."

Salter shook his head. "No way. You're all I've got. You haven't even finished the questioning yet."

Pickett, feeling cornered, said, "I'll finish the block, then. After that I'll go back to my unit."

"I don't know, Mel. What about this friend of Thomas's you were going to interview tomorrow?"

"That's what I mean! Maybe she'll be able to tell you who Abe is. Probably the local bishop that she was screwing Friday afternoons. Another sensitive one. You should do that. We're liable to miss something if we split the case. Something could fall in the cracks."

"What I hear you saying is you don't want to do it."

"No, no. I just think it's risky. For you."

"I think it's bullshit, but all right, I'll look after the riend. You finish the questioning, then we'll see. I'm ot sending you back yet."

Pickett felt defeated. All he'd managed to do was ake over the foot-slogging, leaving the possible jam o Salter. His only recourse now was to quit on the pot, but that was so unprofessional that Salter would now there was something going on. "I'll be in the ffice," Pickett said, trying to sound brisk and disinerested.

Alone in his office, Salter went back to brooding bout his own world. He was not sorry that Pickett ad given him an excuse to take the case over himself. The psychologist was away for a few days, doing his omework in the criminology center at the university, nd the case would fill in the gaps between wondering what was happening to his marriage, what to do about t, and when to do it.

SEVEN

"I'VE GOT A PROBLEM," Salter said. He and his wife, Annie, were sitting in their brand-new kitchen after supper. They were alone; Angus, their elder son, was backpacking around Europe with his girlfriend before they moved on to university; their younger son, Seth, had recently discovered a taste for running, and he spent most of the early evenings plodding around the streets of Toronto. Salter had finished loading the dishwater, and Annie had made up her mind who their eight real friends were and programmed their numbers into the new telephone.

"You listening?" he inquired.

"I'm listening. You've got a problem. Go on. The psychologist?" She squinted along the countertop, then rubbed at a spot with a dishcloth. The new kitchen had displaced the front or living room, and the back of the house had been extended to accommodate a new living room, leaving space in the middle for a hall and a dining room. The kitchen was large and handsome and it allowed them to eat the family meals while they watched the world go by on the street. It also allowed the neighbors to watch them if they forgot to close the blinds. Salter liked the new arrangement; for Annie the kitchen was the biggest toy she had ever had, and she never stopped playing with it, polishing the new wooden cabinets, mopping the quarry tiles on the floor, adjusting the adjustable halogen lamps, arranging the spices alphabetically, then in sets according to whether they were in jars or cans or little plastic bags.

"Not him, no. He's just decided the trouble lies with middle management."

"Meaning?"

"Inspectors and superintendents. He has this theory that middle managers are of two kinds: those who look after the people they work for, and those who look after the people who work for them. Upper management prefers the first kind, but the workers—sergeants and constables—like the second. Are you following this? His theory is that cops, being naturally fascist bastards, always become the first kind when they are promoted, so all the sergeants and constables hate our guts because we are always pissing on them while we are kissing the asses of the deputy chiefs. He's designing a whole new questionnaire to prove his theory. Part of it is that constables on court duty are all embittered because they have been passed over for promotion. I'm going to make sure he interviews Joe Wilkinson."

"I need another shelf," Annie said. "I'd like to put all the jugs together." She looked up. "Sorry. Go on. Why...Joe Wilkinson?" she brought out in triumph, showing how closely she was attending.

"Because they tried to promote Joe three times, to my knowledge, but he won't have it. Says he can't afford promotion. He makes more money with his supplementary payments for court duty than I do. The happiest man on the force."

Annie made a further effort. "Will he question your new man? Is that the problem?"

"Probably, but that's not the problem. It's Pickett himself. *He's* the problem."

"I thought you liked the look of him." Her dutiful interlude over, Annie began again to wander around the room, flicking at unseen dust.

"He's fine at the job. Cute old bastard. But let me tell you. I got a query the other day, a girl looking for a relative about his age. Guy who was in the Air Force in England during the war."

"What kind of relative?"

"That's the point. Sit down for a minute, will you? I think she's looking for her grandfather. She doesn't know his name."

Annie stopped polishing the stove and sniggered.

"What's the joke?"

"A story my uncle used to tell. His favorite line overheard in the blackout in London."

"Which was?"

Annie tried for a cockney accent. "W'minit. I'll take me knickers off, then we can do it prop'ly." She giggled. "Sorry. So what's the problem?"

"I asked Mel Pickett if he knew anyone who fitted the description."

"And?"

"He said he'd think about it. Then I checked the records. It's him."

"Oh, dear."

"Right. See?" Was it his imagination, or had she lost interest in him and his job?

"But she's not entitled to know, is she, if he doesn't want her to? You could pass on the message and forget about it."

"Think about it. If she had come in with his name, I could have passed him the message and he could have done what he liked about it. But it came to me the other way around. So now I know it's him, and why she's looking for him, and he knows I know and soon he'll have figured out that I've guessed who it is. What I'm doing now is pretending not to know."

"How did he react?"

"He looked shocked. You know. He didn't react at all."

"You sure he knows you know?"

"Oh, Christ, yes. Half an hour after I told him he came back into the office and wanted me to take him off the job. Said it was too sensitive for him. He just wanted out, away from me."

"Can't you leave it at that?"

"I don't think so. This kid's determined. She'll find him some way or other."

"So far you've just been guessing he's her grandfather, haven't you?"

"Have you been listening?"

"Your tale, sir, would cure deafness."

"What?"

"Never mind. Tell him. Tell him you've realized."

"Balls to that."

"What are you going to do, then?"

"Stay dumb. Arrange for them to meet, and stay out of the way."

"He may not be pleased."

"I don't know what the hell else to do. Besides, I think he should get a look at this kid. One look may be enough. You should see her."

"He may think you're meddling."

"I'm trying *not* to meddle."

"I see that, Charlie. I hope *he* does."

Just then the dishwasher blew up. There was a large bang, three small pops, an intense blue flame, then a lot of smoke.

"God, what did you do?" Annie said, instinctively and immediately, as Salter pointed out later.

"Nothing. Bloody nothing." Salter leaped about, trying to remember how to deal with electrical fires, but the commotion was over in a few seconds, leaving a small cloud of smoke and a smell of burning. Salter switched the machine, already stopped, to "OFF."

Annie was distraught. As well as the dishwasher there was a new stove, a microwave oven, and a lighting system operated by a panel of switches that glowed in the dark. At night, or very early in the morning, with all the digital clocks and other instruments glowing, the kitchen looked like the control cabin of a vessel commanded by someone with a taste for Old Ontario pine. And now Salter had broken it already.

"You must have done *something*," she said.

"All I fucking well did was put the dishes in the way Carmella showed me." Carmella was their cleaning lady who spoke little English but knew how to operate her client's technology.

"Did you read the manual?"

"What manual?"

Annie reached up to the shelf of cookbooks. "There," she said, handing him three thick magazine-type books. "The microwave, the stove, the dishwasher. Read them. Find out how they work."

Salter stared at the books in fury. They had owned a VCR for a year, and he still couldn't figure out how to program it to record. "All I did was load the dishes in, I poured the soap in the little hole like it says, set the dial to 'Wash'—Low energy, right?—and switched it on. I didn't do anything else. Nothing."

"Read the manuals. I'll call the service department tomorrow."

"Screw the goddamn manuals," he said and hurled the books at the table where they landed, bounced, and slid off the other side. He sat down and huddled in a tense knot, facing the window.

After a few moments Annie picked up the manuals and put them back on the shelf. She sat down at the table at right angles to Salter. "What's the matter?" she asked carefully, paying serious attention to his outburst.

He was afflicted by the difficulty of trying to find the words to break it open. Fear of what was coming mixed with his misery. But it was started now. "What do you think is the matter?" was the best he could do.

"I don't know, Charlie. You look as if you want to hit something. Me?"

"That might help."

She looked at the table between them. "It's serious, then. Should I make some tea before we start? Or do you want to get it over with?"

Two or three times in their marriage there had been scenes like this, but this was the first time he had had the experience of being threatened. Every second that passed helped toward dealing with it in a measured way. "I need a drink," he said. He poured some scotch into a glass and added water from the tap, tasted the drink, and found he had used hot water. He poured the drink away and sat down again.

"What I would like to know," he said, not looking at her, "is what you do on Tuesday nights, who with, and what I'm supposed to do about it."

Now Annie got up. "Can we go in the other room? I don't want to talk out here."

"Why?"

"Because I don't. Can we go into the living room, please? What was wrong with the drink?"

"It tasted soapy," he said, rejecting the farcial truth in favor of an answer that could be a criticism of her dishwasher.

"I'll make another. For both of us."

When they were settled down again, she said, "Someone's been telling stories. Who?"

"No one's been telling stories. Two people have seen you running around. With some guy."

"Have they? Running around with some guy."

"Eating at Sisi's, and at the Harbourfront, listening to some poet."

"Who?"

"One was Blostein."

"Jiri? Our doctor?"

"That's right. When he was looking at my ear he asked me how I liked the restaurant."

"Did he see who I was with?"

"No, or he wouldn't have asked me. He must have seen you going in or coming out. He assumed it was me."

"That's all right, then, isn't it? And the other?"

"The other was Peggy Martin. She called up to see how we'd enjoyed the poet. Asked me who that gorgeous guy was with us."

"Us again. So no one else thinks I'm running around. Just you. Did you tell them you weren't with me?"

"No."

"So *that's* all right."

"Are you having an affair?" It was out now, said. They could not slide past it.

It took her long enough to reply, and Salter ought to have taken warning. Instead he simply braced himself for the news.

"I *have* been seeing someone else, yes. On Tuesday nights. Five or six times."

"Who?"

"Marcello Mastroianni. What does it matter?"

"It matters to me, for Christ's sake. Have you been sleeping with him?"

Once again there was a pause. "No, I have not slept with him."

She was telling the truth, he knew. "So what's going on? I thought you were supposed to be studying Italian with your pals on Tuesdays. Was that just a front?"

"Have you asked any of them about it?" Her voice was sharp.

"I'm asking you. No, I haven't."

"That's something, too, then. All right, let me tell you. Our little Italian group broke up at Christmas. As you know, we had a tutor and we used to meet in one of their houses for conversation."

"You never met here."

She ignored that. "His name is Giuseppe Calle. He's about thirty-five, very good-looking, and he teaches Italian literature at the university. But he only has a part-time job and he gets starvation wages, so he supplements his income with night school and tutoring. Vita heard of him and he agreed to tutor us. The group broke up because the others got discouraged, but I was pleased with the way I was doing so I asked him if he would tutor just me. He said he would, and then he made a better suggestion. Why didn't we spend the evening at an art gallery or a museum or something like that and we could speak Italian while we were together? So we did. We've seen an Italian movie, we've been to an art gallery, we went to Harbourfront to hear an Italian author read. That night we got invited to a reception at the Italian Cultural Institute afterward. That was great. Once we went to hear an Italian movie director give a talk on her films. And once, at my request, we had dinner, for which I paid, which makes him a gigolo or something, I guess."

"And is that it?"

"Is that what?"

"Don't do that. You know what I mean. Why didn't you tell me?"

"Now you've got me worried. I'm not sure. Because I didn't want to be cross-examined about it. Because it would sound funny. Because he was very good-looking. Because I didn't tell you right away and then I didn't want to explain afterward why I didn't tell you right away."

"So there *is* something going on."

"Yes, but not the way you mean."

"What, then?"

"I wasn't ready for this tonight. Wait a minute." She went out to the kitchen, where he could hear her blowing her nose. She reappeared with a glass of water which she set beside her untouched drink.

"It wasn't just the Italian lessons. But I wouldn't have gone with him without the lessons. It was because he talks to me."

"What do you mean, talks to you? In Italian, right?"

"More than that. I mean he talks to me and I talk back. What's new? Read any good books lately? Things. You see, I don't hear us talking much around here lately, except about your job. I feel shrunken lately, and I couldn't resist the chance to see some of the stuff that's going on in Toronto and talk about it. Try this: When was the last time I suggested a movie and you said, 'Great, let's go'? I did feel a bit funny about Sisi's, I admit, so I called you at work a couple of days afterward and suggested we go out for dinner. Remember what you said?"

"I said we could go. But not that night, that's all."

"That's what you've been saying for some time now. 'Yes, but not tonight.' I can't remember the last time you called me at work and said you would pick me up and we'd go out."

"There's the kids."

"The kids have been able to get their own dinner for the past three years."

"I like coming home, to eat here, with you."

"So do I, most of the time."

"I thought the house was working well." He waved toward the kitchen. "We had this out years ago. I try to do my share."

"I know you do. I'm not complaining about that."

"What is it, then? I'm dull. Boring. That it?"

"That's not fair." And then she became bright-eyed as she sought, angrily, not to cry. "You're not dull and boring, but *we* could be if you don't do something about it. Why wouldn't you go to that square-dancing party last week?''

"I didn't know it was that important. I'd've gone." He wished desperately now that he had.

"No, you wouldn't. Not unless we had had this row. You thought it was a lot of imitation cowboys prancing about in check shirts, didn't you? You didn't want to look a fool. You didn't think it might be fun, did you? Okay, so you don't want to go square dancing. That's all right. But you're the same with everything. I've stopped making suggestions. You are the same on the island, in the summer. You won't let my family teach you about sailing or anything because you're afraid you'll be at a disadvantage. All they want to do is include you. You just go off and play golf and I have to run back and forth between you all. You're a pig, sometimes, and I'm not sure I can take it for the rest of my life. I'm studying bloody Italian because you and I had a lovely holiday by accident four years ago when you wanted to find out something in Tuscany. Remember? You decided you liked Italy so we had a wonderful time like a honeymoon and I thought we could go back this year and I asked you and you said you didn't know if you could get away and I know you can and so here we are again on this bloody business of your job your job your job night and day and weekends and all you want to do is work and come home and watch television and though you're crabby about that, too, you'd rather read magazines and jump on me Sunday mornings. Oh, shit, I shouldn't have said that. I'm sorry."

"You want me to quit my job?"

She shook her head.

"Because I'm not going to do that. It's going well. I'm too busy, sure, but that won't last forever. The last couple of years have been the best I've had since the early days."

"I know." She kept her face turned away. "And you've gone right back into the old pattern. All I do is watch you thinking about work. I didn't mind it once, when the boys were little, because you still had some energy left for us. Now it all goes in your work. I'm glad things are better for you, but they aren't for me."

"What about your job?"

"If you'd been listening lately you'd know that's not anything anymore. The people I work with are as bad as you except they drink too much. I don't want their life. I want my own."

Once, in a crisis of fear, Salter had received some advice, which was to find the thing he was most afraid of and take it out and stare at it. "You want to separate?" he asked.

For answer she waved blindly at him, still not looking, and he moved over beside her. Then she leaned back away from him and went to work with some tissues on her face. "Seth will be back in a minute," she said.

"Come up to the bedroom. To talk."

She shook her head. "I don't want to talk anymore now."

"Are you going to see this guy again?"

Once more she shook her head, dabbing and sniffing, not in negation, but in withdrawal.

"We can go to Italy." It was all he could think of.

"It doesn't matter that much."

"It looks to me as if it does. Why don't you go to a travel agency tomorrow and book it? Any time from the end of May."

She laughed slightly, then still weeping, she said, "Why don't *you* go? You know I want to go. Come home tomorrow with the tickets."

This was better. "Shall I rent a car?"

"Surprise me."

"That won't work. You know what you want to do. You've been thinking about it. I could come back with a bicycle tour of Naples when you've got your mind set on Rome. I'll go along with anything. I'll fix the dates and I'll pick up some brochures from the Alitalia office and then tomorrow night you tell me what to do next. Okay?"

There was the sound of Seth fumbling with the front door, and Annie jumped up. "Let's talk about it later."

But later, when he finally went up to bed after thinking his way through his married life and drinking a quarter of a bottle of scotch, Annie was asleep. When he climbed in beside her she stirred and reached out and touched him, then turned back to sleep. He hadn't lost her yet, but he needed help.

EIGHT

THE WOMAN WHO OPENED the door to Salter the following morning was still suffering from the news of her friend's death. She turned away from him as he identified himself, stepping back to let him in the door, but he had already noticed the tissues in her hand and the raw patches around her eyes.

She led him through a sitting area, where a ring of armchairs and squashy-looking ottomans surrounded a single glass-topped coffee table. The interior walls had been removed, but between the living space and the kitchen a line of varnished pine uprights separated the two areas. An open wooden staircase rose to the second floor, which had been cut back to a single room over the kitchen with a row of pine beams hung with pots of flowers, replacing the old ceiling over the living room. Salter chose the one chair with a high back, feeling the need for something solid in all this architectural space. The woman supplied herself with some fresh tissues from a box on the coffee table and sat down across from him, waiting.

"Sheila Barnsley?"

She nodded and blew her nose.

"You were a friend of Linda Thomas?"

"Yes, I was. Am. Was."

There was still some grief to get through, and Salter waited for her to compose herself. "Can you tell me something about her? What did she call herself, a massage therapist?"

"That's what she was. She wasn't licensed, but she was very good. I referred a couple of people to her. I just hope to God it wasn't one of those I referred who killed her."

"Was she trained?"

"Yes, but not in Ontario. In the States. That's why she didn't have a license to practice here."

"Who were the people you referred to her?"

She gave him two names, and Salter looked through his notebook. "We've checked them both. They're not involved."

The woman made a face indicating relief.

"What do you do, Miss Barnsley?"

"For a living? I'm a psychotherapist."

"What's that?"

"I help people with personal problems."

"You talk to them?"

"That's right."

"You're a psychologist? A psychiatrist?"

"Neither. I'm a therapist. I have no formal qualifications."

"Where do your clients come from?"

"Word of mouth. I get referrals—from psychologists, among others. And other clients."

"Why would you send people on to Miss Thomas?"

"Because they are tense. My clients usually suffer from stress, which shows up physically, and sometimes relieving the physical tension is a beginning to relieving the whole problem."

"You knew Miss Thomas very well?"

"Very. I told you. I met her in a therapy group I was in. About ten years ago. Because of that group I took up psychotherapy, to help others. She did the same thing, but she got more interested in massage therapy."

"Miss Barnsley, it has been suggested that she might have gone beyond massage, which would be a help to know."

"Oh, for God's sake." She looked away from him in an elaborate gesture of disgust. She looked back at him accusingly, then continued. "Sex, you mean. No. Not in a thousand years. She was very careful who she took on, and very clear to them about what she was doing. We talked about it. I've done some massage, and I know the problem. Say 'massage' and everyone thinks 'parlors,' 'fifty-dollar hand jobs.' She knew all about that. She worked in a downtown hotel at first until she got tired of being taken for a prostitute by all the visiting firemen. After that she worked at a sports club, and this time it was the locals who propositioned her. So she went into private practice, strictly referrals, and then it was okay. She was building up a practice slowly—she couldn't advertise without a license and she probably wouldn't have anyway, for the same reasons I've just told you, and she still did typing."

"However careful you are—let's say she was—isn't massage liable to be misunderstood? It's pretty intimate."

"Sometimes a client gets a whatdyoucallit, a hardon? An erection? It happens. But if your client is there for medical reasons, he's going to be embarrassed. Like being turned on by a nurse. So you leave the room until he's over it. No problem. It happened a couple of times to her. We laughed about it. You know, 'poor guy.' Most men are more afraid of reacting than we are of them. That's why they go to a woman, a masseuse."

"Huh?"

"Homophobia, Inspector. Fear of being turned on by a man."

There was some attempt to disturb Salter in the aggressive tone of her replies, a temporary (he hoped) disgust for men, which perhaps Thomas's killer had brought out. He moved on. "We checked every name in her appointment book and accounted for them all except one."

"Abe?"

Salter laid his notebook on the arm of his chair and nodded. "That's the name. Who is he? Do you know?"

She shook her head. "I don't think it's possible. She's known him for months. She told me all about him. He wasn't her client. They were lovers. Why would he kill her?''

Salter's experience included more than one case of men who had suddenly, without reason or cause, slaughtered their families and then turned themselves over to the police; good, gray men, with hobbies and no history of any kind of violence. ''We have to check him out,'' Salter said. ''Who is he?''

''I don't know. I know all about him, though. He's married, and he and Linda were having an affair. They used to meet about every two weeks. She wouldn't tell me anything about him in case I let it slip out. He was such a well-known figure that he would have been ruined if anyone had found out. I sometimes thought he must have been a minister—you know, a clergyman. Who else would lose his job over an affair these days? Man, I mean.''

Tell me he's a bishop, Salter thought. Make Pickett's day. ''And that's all you know about him?''

''Yes.'' The woman, more relaxed now, looked at him doubtfully. ''Surely the person who killed her must have been someone off the street? Someone who got into her apartment?''

''We're checking. Do you know anything more about this Abe? Did she ever mention where he came from? Was he Canadian? Was he black? Was he from a different culture? Young? Old? Did he drink? Was he a vegetarian? Big? Thin? Did he smell good? Did he wear glasses? If she talked about him at all she must have given you some hints, however careful she was. Anything.''

She shook her head. ''I think he must have been ordinary. White. I mean, Canadian, stuff like that. She wouldn't talk about him, like he was a sacred subject. I always thought his secret was safe with her. The only reason I found out about him was I tried to fix her up with a blind date once and she said she didn't need a blind date. And then to avoid being rude, she told me she had a lover. I wondered if she was making him up at first, but then something happened that convinced me. I was in her apartment; the phone rang and she was changing, so I answered it. Some man. I told him to hang on, but he just said tell her Dr. Mackane called, and hung up. I gave her the message through the bedroom door and she came out all flustered and said she'd have to stay home until he called back, and would I mind leaving her alone after all. We were supposed to be going out together and I was a bit peed off, but I thought maybe she was waiting for the result of some test she didn't want to talk about, so I never pushed it. But she never told me what it was about, which I thought kinda strange. We shared all the usual women's fears, breast cancer, stuff like that. So then I thought that Dr. Mackane was probably Abe.''

''Thanks.'' Salter stuffed his notebook in his pocket and reached for his raincoat. ''Was she a timid person?'' he asked on his way out. ''Did she always put the chain on her door?''

"She always kept it locked, but I don't remember her fiddling about with chains when I called. I don't think she was timid, or afraid beyond the ordinary. She wasn't silly. I would say she felt secure enough with the buzzer system and the spyhole in her door. She probably put the chain on at night, and she probably felt, as I do, that it's kind of old-maidish to lock and bar yourself in all the time, but maybe there really are ten times as many rapists around as there used to be. It seems that way sometimes."

Salter waited for her to open the door for him. "Give this some thought, will you, Miss Barnsley? See if you can come up with anything else about this Abe guy." He smiled. "As you say he was probably in church conducting a wedding that afternoon, but I need to tick him off the list."

THE FIRST STEP WAS EASY. He looked through Linda Thomas's appointment book and found the entry he was hoping for: "Dr. Mackane," dated six months before. Thereafter he found two more entries at intervals of two weeks, then they stopped, but two weeks later the first "Abe" entry occurred, then recurred regularly until the afternoon of her death. The one unhelpful peculiarity was the absence of a telephone number. The next stop ought to have been easy, too: The spelling was unusual, and it was simply a matter of checking through the medical directories, but here his investigation came to a dead end. None of the directories, not even the telephone directory, listed the name.

"Using a false name?" he wondered aloud to Pickett, who had called in to his office to report.

"You wouldn't *make up* a name, would you? You'd pick one that sounded likely. She spell it wrong, maybe?"

"Three times. She would have asked him."

"Out of town?"

"I'll start looking. I'll try Ontario first."

"Then New York State and Michigan. Americans go in for made-up names. You know, three generations back some immigration official at Ellis Island heard it that way and that's what the family got called. It might not be Scotch. Chinese, maybe. Mah Koon, something like that."

"Take another look around that apartment. If they were lovers there ought to be some sign of it. We weren't looking for a name before."

Pickett nodded and prepared to leave. As he reached the door, Salter said, "That girl was back." He held up the note to indicate who he meant. "Had any ideas yet?"

"None."

Salter waited for more.

"I was thinking," Pickett said. "Does this kid have the right to know, even if we find her relative? What if the guy doesn't want to be bothered? What does she say he is—great-uncle or second cousin or something? If you do find him, ask him first if he wants to be known."

"She's a funny kid." Salter stood up and fiddled with the venetian blind as he talked. "She thought of that. She didn't tell me how she thinks they're related. She said she doesn't want to embarrass him if he doesn't want to know her. She just wants to give him a message and let him take it from there. As I said, I suspect she's looking for her grandfather."

"If I think of anyone, I'll tell you."

ALREADY, by not immediately suggesting himself, Pickett had created an awkward situation should he want to change his mind, but he was not yet ready to deal with this girl and her revelation. At this stage of his career and given the freedom of the times, there was nothing to be lost professionally. Even the moral disapproval of a senior officer would be irrelevant. Pickett's only problem lay in wondering what would happen if he lifted the veil between himself and this child. If he acknowledged her as his natural grandchild, what then? He found himself wondering now about what his own response would be if it were happening to someone else. He was going to have to make up his mind soon, because the longer he kept silent the more difficult it would be to speak and he would have to prepare himself for the possibility that Salter would realize who the girl's relative was without any help from Pickett.

He spent the rest of the morning and half the afternoon trudging around the apartment block, finding
mostly old people home in the daytime. Several of
them knew the woman, and several more had heard of
her; that is, they knew there was a masseuse on the
block and they wondered at first if she was one of
those you read about in the papers, a small cloud of
gossip that Pickett thought could probably all be
traced back to the janitor's wife. This apart, none of
the tenants had anything to offer him, except one, who
told him about a car that used to sit outside the block
for hours until one day she saw a police car stop by the
car and a policeman talk to the driver, but it couldn't
have been anything serious because the man still came
back.

"And that's it," Pickett said to Salter. "I'll have to
check the rest at night, when they get home from
work. So far I've run into one woman acting a little
strange. She didn't want to talk to me, even after I
showed my card. Treated me like one of those relig-
ious nuts who go door to door. She didn't know anything. Never saw anything, never heard of the woman,
all in ways to make me wonder. I'll check her out. She
might just be frightened of the cops. As for the guy in
the car, there's a record of the incident. Name's Spike,
Colin Spike. Owns a photo shop on the Danforth. I'll
go and see him."

"I'll do it." Salter made a note of the address. "Stay
with the questioning."

Pickett nodded. "There was a road crew outside all Friday afternoon. I'll talk to them, and then I'll hit up all the neighbors."

Salter was glad to be getting out of the office. Keeping an eye on the psychologist, monitoring his questions, was both extremely boring and a considerable strain, like watching a radar screen for the fatal blip that means trouble.

Danforth Avenue was only a couple of minutes away, and it took him ten more minutes to park after he found Spike's camera store. The shop occupied a frontage just large enough for a door and a small display unit. The door opened onto a narrow space in front of the counter. Behind the counter a man with a "wanted" face—lank black hair hanging over one eye, the look of having been punched out recently—was attending to an automatic photo printing machine that took up most of the space in the store. Salter looked around the room, waiting for the print run to end. The glass counter contained four or five cameras and a lot of accessories, and on the back wall several tripods had been hung in display. Salter guessed that this was largely window dressing: this was a neighborhood store whose main business was processing and selling film.

The owner switched off the machine and looked sideways at Salter. "You want something?" he asked, a challenge as much as an inquiry.

"Spike?"

"Unless you want money, yes."

"Just a few words." Salter showed his card.

Spike stayed on his stool. "Last Friday afternoon I was here in the shop from twelve o'clock until six. The janitor found her at half past five. Right?"

"How do you know?"

"I asked him as soon as I heard the news. I knew you'd be 'round. I'm a very suspicious character."

"Anyone see you here?"

"Here's a list of the phone numbers of all the customers I served that afternoon. It takes about twenty-five minutes each way to get from here to her place. About an hour altogether. I'd have to close up the shop, but I didn't."

"You told the patrol car you were waiting for your daughter. You said she had been playing hockey and you knew she had a boyfriend in the area so you went looking for him."

"That's right. That's what I said."

"Is that true?"

"No. I haven't got a daughter. Good story, though, wasn't it?"

"It worked. They believed you. So what were you doing?"

"Waiting." Spike flung himself off the stool and lifted a flap on the end of the counter. "Come back here and I'll tell you the story." He pointed Salter to a chair behind the printing machine. "Here it is, then. I wasn't waiting for Linda. I was waiting for her boyfriend. Guy who teaches at the university. He was the one I was waiting for."

"Why?"

"He took her away from me. About a month ago. We were at a party and she was supposed to go home with me. She went home with him instead. I don't like looking like a fool."

"So you waited outside her apartment block, hoping to catch him?"

"That's right. He had to come by eventually."

"How long—how often did you wait?"

"When I wasn't in the store, I was there."

"For a month?"

"Three weeks. Until last Friday."

"What's his name?"

"Hayes, David Hayes. Professor."

"Where?"

"University of Toronto. He didn't do it, either. He was giving a seminar that afternoon."

"You already checked?"

"Yeah, I thought he might've done it, but he didn't."

"You've got his number?"

Spike went to a list of numbers scribbled on a sheet of paper taped to the wall and read one off.

"What was your connection with her?"

"We were in the same dance exercise class. Hayes was, too. The class had a party and I understood she was with me, but she went home with him, like I said."

"And for that you were going to pound him?"

"Yeah."

"And now?"

"No point now, is there."

Spike pushed the flap of hair out of his eyes and lit another cigarette, the third since Salter had arrived. "All right?" he asked. "Can I go now?" he added, not deferentially.

"Did you see anybody you knew going into that block while you were watching it?"

"If I had I would've told you without being asked. No, I never even saw her."

"Would you look at some pictures for me sometime?"

"Sure. I didn't take much notice, though. It was Hayes I was looking for."

"Someone else might have registered. If you saw a picture you might remember a face."

"Bring them 'round, then."

"Another thing: Was there someone called Abe in your group?"

"Not while I was. Sorry."

"Did you ever hear the name? Did she ever mention it?"

"She was a therapist, wasn't she? Supposed to be confidential?" Now Spike began to move around Salter, pressing to be allowed to get on with his work. Salter walked back around the counter. "Where does your exercise class meet?" he asked.

"Threadneedle Street. I wouldn't bother, though. We've met since then. None of the others knows anything about her."

"Was Hayes there?"

"No, but he didn't do it. I talked to him."

"That's him and you off the list, then, isn't it?"

HAYES, SALTER WAS MADE to understand, was embarrassed by the situation he found himself in. The death of the girl was the biggest embarrassment, of course, but knowing Spike was embarrassing, too, as was belonging to a dance class.

They were sitting in Hayes' office, overlooking a patch of grass used for outdoor exercises. A madman, heavy weights attached to his ankles, was trying to run around the perimeter of the patch, sweat pouring down his face. Hayes bustled to make Salter welcome, even coming out from behind his desk and joining Salter on the broken couch under the window. A simple question had been enough to provoke a smiling, self-deprecating monologue, minimalizing Hayes' connection with Linda Thomas.

"I joined the exercise class and she was there, as was our friend, Spike. An eclectic group. After the class we went our separate ways."

"But you did go to the party. The one you took her home from?"

"Guilty of that, yes." Hayes made a long downward swooping motion of his head. "And of accepting her offer for a trial massage. But that was all."

"It was enough to get Spike mad."

"Ah-ah. He told you, did he?"

"He told me he planned to pound you."

Hayes tried to roar with laughter. "Yes, yes. Black-and-white world our friend Spike lives in. But that's by the way now, I should have thought."

"You were in her apartment a couple of times. Can you tell me anything about her private life?" And sit still? Salter thought. The man seemed to require a different arrangement of limbs for every sentence.

"Not a thing, I'm afraid. She was very properly discreet."

"Did anyone else in your group take her out?"

"Not that I am aware of. But I scarcely did myself. Spike thinks he did, of course."

"You never saw her meet anyone after the work-out?"

Hayes considered this carefully. "No," he said finally. "The only clue I can offer you"—he paused for a long second—"is Abe."

Salter pretended a routine interest. "Abe who?" he asked, writing it down. "Who is Abe?"

Now the head swooping began again. "I would *guess* that he is someone she was emotionally attached to." He changed into a narrative voice. "I was waiting for her in the living room one Sunday afternoon—we were going to a lecture at the Metro Library, and there was a book on her coffee table, *Three Men in a Boat*. You know it, of course?"

Salter shook his head.

"It's a very famous comic story about a boating expedition on the Thames in England. Now, the thing was, the book was brand new and every copy I've ever seen is dog-eared. So I picked it up to see when it was printed and inside the cover was the inscription 'From Abe, with Love.' When she came out of the bedroom I remarked on the book and she took it away from me quickly and put it on her bookshelf. I didn't mention the inscription, of course, or ask her who 'Abe' was.''

"When was this?"

"A month ago. No more."

Salter scratched his chin. "Now tell me what you were doing on Friday afternoon."

Hayes went to his desk and thumbed through his diary. "Friday," he said. "Friday. Here we are. On Friday," he said with a casualness so contrived that Salter wondered how he had kept the information to himself for so long, "I delivered a lecture to my colleagues on 'Narrative and Discourse in the Films of John Huston.' That's the director. That was at two o'clock. Afterward there was a reception, which lasted until four-thirty. Then I went with some of my graduate students for a drink, until about six." Hayes looked queryingly at Salter with an air of fake tentativeness, as if he had no idea how watertight it was.

Salter suspected that Hayes' interest in Thomas had been more than casual, though not reciprocated. Nevertheless, he was off the hook, but he supplied, possibly, a useful lead, justifying Salter's afternoon. The policeman shook hands with him reassuringly and left for Thomas's apartment.

NINE

HE WENT ALONG THE SHELVES, opening the books one by one, looking at the inscriptions. All of them were identified simply with her name and the date she had bought the book, until he came to *Three Men in a Boat*. There, in a neat, clerkly hand, was the inscription. Salter continued along the shelves and found two more, both paperbacks, the first, *The Collected Patrick Campbell*, similarly inscribed, and the second, *The Thurber Carnival*, inscribed "To Linda, with regards, Abraham Mackane." The handwriting in all three was the same, and there was one other bonus: When he flicked open *The Collected Patrick Campbell*, a thin card fell out, a bookmark printed "The Scriveners' Company," a bookstore on Yonge Street not far from where Salter lived. He tucked the books into the pockets of his raincoat, happy that Abe and Mackane were the same man, feeling certain now of tracking him down.

The tiny assistant behind the counter at "The Scriveners' Company" looked at him warily, like a kitten peeping out of a shoe. Salter explained himself and handed the books to her. She looked at the minuscule notation in the corner of each flyleaf and handed them back. "Yes. They are all ours."

"Could you tell me when you sold them and who to?"

She blinked at him, then disappeared into the back of the store. A cheerful giantess in a denim dress and wearing huge sandals emerged with the books in her hand. She looked like the mother hen of the day-old chick, her assistant. "'Twould be virtually impossible to establish the date of purchase of any of them," she said, in what sounded to Salter like a West Indian accent, something to do with the precise formality of the syntax and the tinkling sound of the consonants. "I couldn't even approximate the time of the first two. But I might guess when the Patrick Campbell was sold. 'Twas the last copy on the shelf, and since I always reorder immediately, I can say with certainty that it was between February the fifteenth and the twenty-second that it left the store. May I ask why you want to know?"

"We're trying to find out who bought them."

"*The Case of the Homicidal Bibliomaniac?* Let me see who wrote up the bill." She disappeared into the back room and emerged within two minutes. "Frederick it was, a student who works here some afternoons. He may remember because he is addicted to Patrick Campbell and probably engaged the customer in conversation. Frederick's at the university now, but he will be in later. Let me inquire and call you. Have you got a card?"

She called back that afternoon. "Frederick is here now. Hold on, please."

"Frederick Zichy here."

"You remember the man you sold the book to?"

"It's rather fading. An older man, forty or fifty, thin, very pleasant. Bought it for someone else, because he already knew the stories. What else?"

"Glasses?"

"I think not."

"Nothing about his clothes?"

"No."

"Tall?"

"Medium."

"Any accent?"

"Not that I remember."

"You talked about the book. Remember what he said? Anything? Why was he buying it?"

"He was buying it for someone else. He couldn't find a copy in Marlborough, where he lived."

"You sure he lives in Marlborough?"

"No. I'm sure he *said* he did."

"That's very precise. Thank you, Frederick. Now, give me your phone number and address."

It took Salter one call to the Ontario Provincial Police in Marlborough and a wait of three minutes to learn that Dr. Abraham Mackane was the president of Marlborough University.

"JESUS CHRIST," Pickett said. "A deputy minister, a TV personality, and now a college president. Sensitive is right. You sure he's the right guy?"

"It's a rare name."

"I'd have expected him to be in touch with us, through a lawyer, if he's in the clear."

"They were lovers. He doesn't realize his name was in her book."

"How you going to handle it?"

"Carefully. Drive down. Ask to see him in private. Don't show my card unless I have to. Play it by ear then, as I tell him what I know and what I want to know from him."

"You won't need me, will you? I haven't finished with the neighbors yet."

"No, stay on the block. I'll bring back a picture of this guy in case we need you to find someone to identify him."

Pickett nodded and left the office happy. The girl seemed to have faded, and with Salter out of the way he planned to take a little side trip before he started work the next day. He wanted to have a look at Black Creek Pioneer Village, a collection of early Canadian buildings assembled on a site a few kilometers north of Toronto, designed to reproduce something of the atmosphere of nineteenth-century Canadian village life. Some of the buildings are constructed of logs, and he wanted to check the ways in which the logs were joined.

It was the experience of converting his house, working with his hands, using tools, that had ignited his small dream of building a log cabin. There was a cabin in his blood. After his mother died he came across a picture of his great-grandfather, a snapshot of a short, bald pioneer with bad teeth leaning on his ax outside his new home. The combination of a magazine article, a glimpse of a cabin on the French River, and a television program coalesced into a decision, and he confided in his librarian neighbor (and only in her), and she brought home five books on the subject. He read the first chapter of each and learned enough to keep him busy for a year. Near Kinmount he found a piece of land, five acres of bog and trees with a pond, a stream, and a small rocky outcrop, a little plateau that sat dry above the bog. He bought a secondhand house trailer, and on his first real visit cleared enough trees with a chainsaw to be able to park the trailer on the rock. The trailer had a propane stove, a fridge, and two bunk beds, and once he had spent his first night he knew he could pull it off. It would take him several years, but he was in no hurry. He wanted to build a cabin, not live in one, and he could take his time doing it. He cut enough trees the first summer for the walls, and now they had to be stripped, notched, and laid in place. It would soon be dry enough to go up there again. Willis could hardly wait. For her it was paradise without a leash, and she watched for Pickett to put the chainsaw in the hall, ready to be loaded into the car. Thereafter she slept all night next to the saw so as not to be left behind.

TEN

AMERICANS TRAVELING from Detroit to Toronto along Highway 401 can be forgiven for assuming that southwestern Ontario is something of a little England. The names of the major towns—Chatham, London, Woodstock, Kitchener, Waterloo, and of course, Stratford (on Avon)—do their best to create an image of those early English settlers spreading across the fertile country, putting down roots, and naming the places home.

In fact, until the end of the nineteenth century, three quarters of the population of Kitchener were of German origin, beginning with the first Mennonites in 1805. The illusion of Englishness has been helped by the fact that more than one of these towns had another name before 1914. Thus Kitchener was once called Berlin, and Marlborough is the old Munich in disguise.

The town of Marlborough lies just off the highway, between Kitchener and London, and here Salter came first to let the Ontario Provincial Police know he was in their territory and to get directions to the university. Ten minutes from the town hall he pulled up at the gates of the entrance to the campus and asked his way of the security guard. Behind the guard's hut he could see the buildings of the university scattered across a wide landscape, and Salter guessed from his experience at Toronto's "other" university that you could probably drive around in circles for an hour before finding someone who could direct you to the building you were trying to find.

"You want Blenheim Palace," the guard said. "Otherwise known as the Administration Building. That's it." He pointed to the largest of the brick structures directly ahead. "You can't park, though."

"What do I do? Write a message on a stick and throw it through a window as I drive by?"

"You park here. Cost you three dollars."

"I might as well leave it in the road. That building's a quarter of a mile away."

"There's only two places for distinguished visitors behind the building. They let us know each morning if anyone distinguished is expected. No one is today."

Reluctantly, Salter identified himself.

"I suppose you can park there, then. Can I help?"

"I doubt it." He had not meant to sound offensive, but once spoken, the words could not be softened. The guard's face closed. Salter said, "What I mean is, I want to surprise this guy."

"Who?"

"Dr. Mackane."

The guard seemed about to say something; then his face closed again. "Lotsa luck," he said and withdrew into his shack.

Salter drove in, parked his car behind the building, and found his way to a secretary's office, where he explained his business. "It's a private matter," he said to the girl seated at a word processor. He considered how best to keep it that way. "If Dr. Mackane is in, I'd like to see him for a few minutes."

"I'm sorry," the girl began, and Salter pulled out his card.

"Take this into him, will you, and tell him I'll wait for however long it takes until he's free."

Once more the girl started to protest, looking around her for support.

"Are you his secretary?" Salter demanded.

The girl half nodded, as if reluctant to commit herself.

"Then just take in the card and tell him I'm here." He turned away and walked across the office to look at a picture on the opposite wall.

She shrugged and disappeared through a large oak door with Dr. Mackane's name on it in script; a few minutes later the door opened and a middle-aged man emerged, peering over half glasses and shooing the girl in front of him. "Inspector Salter? Come on in, please." He stood back to let Salter in, motioning him to a couch. "We'd better make ourselves comfortable."

"Dr. Mackane?"

"Sit down first. Right. Inspector, Dr. Mackane is not here. He collapsed a month ago, a coronary. He's been under intensive care ever since. If this is completely personal, then perhaps you should be speaking to his wife. She lives in the manse, here on campus. If it is to do with the university, if you are merely calling on 'the president' in pursuit of your inquiries about someone else, I might be able to help you. My name is Koren, Alvin Koren. I am the academic vice president, presently acting president.''

"Why didn't the girl tell me?"

"She said you wouldn't let her. She told me that it is a personal matter and I think she thinks it is none of my business. She is Dr. Mackane's secretary and she is very attached to him, and frankly not very easy for me to work with. Is it? Any of my business?''

Salter found himself without words. He saw immediately what had happened. Linda Thomas had filled in her appointment book in advance, setting aside a regular meeting time for Abe. Salter was wasting his time. He kept it as general as he could. "I'm working on a case in Toronto. Dr. Mackane's name cropped up as someone who might help me."

"If you had called ahead I could have saved you a journey."

"I had to come this way for other stuff. I was just passing the university when I remembered about Dr. Mackane, so I pulled in."

"Two cases that bring you to Marlborough on the same day?" Koren looked wondering, on the edge of disbelief. "Anyway, Dr. Mackane's indisposed. You won't be able to drop in on him, I'm afraid."

"I'm not certain he's the man I want."

"You mean there's some *other* Dr. Mackane? Do you know his first name?"

"Abraham."

"That's the man." Koren looked around the room. "Do you know what your Dr. Mackane looked like?" He moved over beside a picture on the wall.

"No. Is that him?"

"Here he is at the sod-turning ceremony for the new library. That was taken last spring."

The picture showed a smiling group standing around 'a man holding a silver-plated shovel. "That's Mackane holding the shovel."

"Can I keep this?"

"I suppose so. I'd like it back sometime. I'll get Brodersen to find you an envelope."

"Are you close to him, sir?"

"Not really. I'm V.P., Academic, so I am close to him in that sense. But we're not friends. We're not enemies, either."

"Is anyone close to him around here? Does a president have friends?"

"You want to ask some personal questions? Fine. I'm not in charge of his secrets. Let me see. Who would know the kind of thing you want to ask about?" He looked at Salter, who felt around his tongue with his teeth, waiting.

When he got no response, Koren said, "Odd as it sounds, I think the best man many be the college services administrator. They play tennis together, and Mackane uses him as a kind of personal assistant. Not for academic matters, of course. Yes, Orchard's the man."

"Orchard?" He wrote the name in his book.

"Tommy Orchard. I'll ask Brodersen to get him for you."

Salter wondered if the dropping of the secretary's title was democratic, gender-neutral, or simply hostile. Koren expressing his dislike of the woman.

Koren spoke into the telephone, giving her the message, and the two men waited. "Is one permitted to inquire farther?" Koren asked after they had sat in silence for several minutes.

"I thought you didn't want to know."

"Oh, I want to know, I just don't want anyone to know that I know."

"How do we manage that?"

"Oh, all right." The door opened and Koren jumped up. "Here he is now." He took the newcomer by the arm and brought him into the room. "Tommy, this is Staff Inspector Salter. He wants to talk to you."

"About Dr. Mackane," Salter said, seeing Orchard look alarmed.

"About Dr. Mackane," repeated Koren. "That much I know, Tommy, and no more. So take the inspector along to your office. Don't tell anyone you meet along the way who he is. After you've finished, bring Mr. Salter back here and we'll have lunch. That suit you, Inspector? The food here is offensive but not inedible."

"I don't need to bother you that far, sir."

"Nonsense. We'll have lunch at high table. My pleasure." Koren spread his arms to indicate the size of his pleasure. "See you later, then." He closed his arms around their shoulders, effectively ejecting them through the door.

TOMMY ORCHARD'S OFFICE seemed very academic until Salter looked around and saw that the shelves were loaded, not with books, but with the catalogs the supervisor needed to purchase the college supplies. The one wall without catalogs was covered with framed photographs of college events in which Orchard had been featured, including the same picture of the sod-turning ceremony Salter had borrowed from Koren. Leaning against the wall in the corner behind the desk, a tennis racquet attested to Orchard's hobby. The supervisor placed a chair for Salter in front of his desk, and the two men sat down.

"Now, Inspector, what can I do for you?" Orchard passed a hand over his ear, pushing his thick yellow hair back in place, and stretched his neck free of his collar.

"I'd like to know what you can tell me about Dr. Mackane. I didn't tell that vice president why I was inquiring because he guessed it might be better if as few people knew as possible, including himself. He may have to know. Depends. How well do you know Dr. Mackane?"

"We are friends, rather good friends."

"Excuse me for wondering, Mr. Orchard, but the president and the guy who buys the supplies? I'd have thought he'd have found his friends among the professors."

"I never went to university, Inspector, so I can't generalize for you. This *is* a very democratic college—they call it 'collegiality'—and the fact is, however surprising, Dr. Mackane and I rubbed along pretty well. I worked for him directly. Normally there would be a vice president for administration, but we aren't big enough to need one. There's a comptroller, a bursar, and me, and we do all the nonacademic stuff among us. Oh, and an engineer."

"You make it sound as though Dr. Mackane isn't coming back."

"That's what people say."

Salter felt an instinct to try to loosen Orchard up. "What's this 'high table' stuff?" he asked, feeling in his pockets for a pencil.

"It's where the faculty eat lunch."

"Where do you eat?"

"I am a member of high table. So is the bursar and the comptroller. Not the engineer."

Salter still pretended to be organizing himself for the real questions. "So you and Dr. Mackane socialize, do you?" He settled himself with his notebook and waited for Orchard to answer so they could begin.

"Not our families. Just him and me. On the court."

"Tennis?"

"Yes. I taught him how to play. We played once or twice a week."

"Don't the other professors play?"

"None of them regularly, that I know of."

Now Salter heard Orchard's slight English accent. "So you played tennis." Salter by now had begun to feel his man. Orchard was on his guard, and Salter guessed that he was preparing to be loyal to his friend, the president. It was possible, too, that Orchard held some notion that the less said the better. Salter got up and walked to the window, trying to look as much as possible like one of the English inspectors he had seen on television mysteries. "What I have to ask you is confidential, Mr. Orchard, and to ask my question I have to tell you something about the inquiry that you must keep to yourself." Christ, he thought, I hope no one else is listening. He swung around. "But I can't beat around the bush. I'm investigating the death of a woman in Toronto, and Dr. Mackane's name has come up. Do you know anything about his private life?"

"I know something," Orchard agreed.

"Do you know of a woman he visited in Toronto?"

"What kind of woman?"

"A massage therapist. Did he ever tell you he visited one of those?"

It took Orchard some time to reply. Then, "Yes," he said. "Yes, I knew about her. I wondered..." his voice dried up momentarily. "Was she in an accident?"

"We think it is a homicide."

Orchard now looked confused. "Someone killed her? When?"

"Last week. What do you know about her and Dr. Mackane?"

Again Orchard was slow to respond, as if he had to search a very old memory. "He was involved with her. Apart from therapy. He told me about her."

"Did he tell you they were lovers?"

Orchard looked uncomfortable, embarrassed. "I understood that."

"How often did they meet?"

"About every two weeks. To my knowledge."

"But you knew all about it. Why? Why did he confide in you?"

"Because I covered for him."

"You mean he'd say he was playing tennis with you and he'd really be in Toronto with this therapist? Supposing his wife dropped by the court? How long does a game take? He'd need an excuse for a few hours, wouldn't he?"

"It was understood that we were playing in Toronto. You can't play here in the winter except to practice in the gym, so we joined a winter club in Toronto."

"That was your story. Did you go with him?"

"Yes. We drove in together."

"*You* played tennis but *he* went off for a massage."

"Not every time. He found one or two other excuses that would take him up by himself. And sometimes he really did play tennis. We both did."

"Did he confide in you about her? Let me put it this way: Was she his little thing on the side? Or did he think it was more serious?"

"She was more important than that. She was very important to him." Orchard was clearly irritated by Salter's attitude. He was defending Mackane now.

"Would he have left his wife for her?"

"Oh, no. No. It was just something marvelous that was happening to him, but he wouldn't have wrecked his life here. I had no fear of that."

"Where did he meet her, do you know?"

Orchard thought about this. "I believe on a train coming from Winnipeg. They got into a conversation and he followed it up."

"How long has it been going on?"

Again Orchard paused while he thought his way back. "Six months, I would say."

Salter made himself look satisfied. "What were you going to say before?" he asked, looking at his watch. "You said you were wondering. What?"

"I just wondered if she had heard that Abe was sick."

"Not unless you told her."

"I didn't know where to find her. I would have."

"He really kept it dark, didn't he?"

There was no response from Orchard, and Salter stood up. "We should be getting back to Professor

Koren. By the way, what's happening to Mackane's personal stuff? From his office?''

"It's all in a box in a closet."

"You have access to it? Good. I'd like to look at his desk diary. Can you dig it out? I don't really need it, but it would tap everything into place if I could match up the appointments with her diary. Did he have a personal diary, too?''

"I imagine so. His wife will have that."

"Let's not bother her unless we have to. It sounds to me as if this isn't going to have any ramifications for her if we can confirm it all from his book.''

"I'll get it for you before you go. We should go to lunch now. The vice president will be waiting."

"Fine. Let's climb up to this high table of yours."

KOREN WAS WAITING for them in the corridor outside his office. "Finished?'' he called as they walked toward him. "Good. Let's join the others at the trough. The dining room is across the green," he said to Salter. "We use the tunnel in bad weather, but I thought we might risk it outside today." He showed the way to a side door and out onto the footpath that led them away from the administration building and across the campus. Dr. Koren pointed out the sights to Salter along the way. Orchard fell in behind them. "Marlborough University was set up in the 1960s," he began. "That's the heating plant over there. To the left is Nelson College. Just a few temporary classrooms really, but we're trying to start the college system here.

That's the women's residence behind it, and over there is The Finnsburgh Fragment." He pointed to what was apparently the facade of an old building supported by four Greek columns, the whole thing preserved like a flat sculpture after the rest of the building had been demolished. "That's an English Department joke. Apparently you have to know Anglo-Saxon." Koren waited for a courteous few seconds in case Salter knew Anglo-Saxon, then continued. "The university is built on land donated by a local brewer of Bavarian extraction, a man named Finnsburgh, who left his house and land for the purpose of starting a college. The house was useless for academic purposes, but we used the land and preserved the front of the house to honor his name."

"So what's the joke?"

"Let me see if I can explain. Apparently there is an Anglo-Saxon manuscript called 'The Finnsburg Fragment.' Don't ask me why. So when they decided to preserve the front of Finnsburgh's house, some wit called it The Finnsburgh Fragment."

"I see. How old is the university?"

"Twenty-three years. We've started preparing for our quarter-centenary celebrations."

"Is Dr. Mackane the second president?"

"Not quite. The first president was a man named Wesley Cowper. He's still with us. President emeritus and professor of political science, he is now, though he doesn't do any actual teaching. He's the director of our Center for Commonwealth Relations, which he set up just before he retired. We don't see too much of him because he spends most of his time at conferences abroad. His successor was a geographer, hired away from us by a milk company to advise them on the best locations for their retail stores. Dr. Mackane is our third president. Not a lot for twenty-three years, but Dr. Cowper, the first man, had a long incumbency."

He looked as if there was more to be said, but they had now arrived at the senior common room, where three others were already awaiting the signal to eat. Koren led him over to a small fat man who was reading a notice board. "This is our bursar, Mr. Sheffield," he said. "Inspector Salter." They shook hands, and Koren led Salter away to a tall, gray-haired lady dressed in a badly dyed Indian-type garment over an embroidered, slightly soiled blouse and a row of wooden beads. She had a look on her face as if she found Salter absurd. "Our poet," Koren said. "Esther Kleinburg. Please welcome Inspector Salter."

"Do I have to call you 'Inspector'?" She peered at him closely, mocking the formality of their situation but not, as far as Salter could tell, him. "What are you inspector of? Can I call you mister?" The last sentence was said within an inch of Salter's nose.

"I'm not in uniform. Sure."

"That's what I'll call you, then. Come and talk to me until they open the door. I'm starving and you can take my mind off it." She put her arm through his and tried to make for a sofa, but Koren clamped onto

Salter's other arm and drew him firmly away toward the third occupant of the room, a jowly man in his late sixties with a tangle of white hair over each ear.

"That's not very nice, Alvin," the poet said. "You introduce me to a lovely new face then whisk him away." It was clearly her style to be outrageous.

Koren smiled tolerantly but continued to draw Salter across the room. "Our most eminent scholar," he hissed in Salter's ear. "Reads ten languages and invents his own computer programs for textual analysis. Ah, Dr. Burns. I'd like you to meet my guest, Inspector Salter."

The eminent scholar shook hands, then the door to the dining room opened and he hurried through first, followed immediately by the others. It reminded Salter of meal call in an open prison.

High table was a single piece of imitation Jacobean oak that stretched from one wall almost to the other on a platform at one end of the dining room. Three feet below, about a hundred undergraduates were already fighting for places around the tables in the main dining space. Koren led Salter to a chair and seated himself beside him as the others took their places. Soon they were joined by four more faculty members, each of whom shook hands with Salter before they sat down. One of them, a young man with a fringe of ginger beard, positioned himself opposite the eminent scholar and got a nod of acknowledgment for his "Good day to you, sir," a form of address Salter had only read, never heard spoken.

A thick, whitish, fishy soup was followed by a small portion of macaroni cooked together with a handful of ground meat to form a stew; the dessert was a hard square of pastry on which applesauce had been poured. A large block of orange-colored cheese surrounded by salted crackers sat on a piece of marble in the center of the table, but only the oldest faculty members bothered with it. When they were well into the soup, the voice of the poet came to Salter from down the table: "You still haven't told us what you are an inspector of, Mr. Salter. Has he, Alvin?"

"Inspector Salter is with the Toronto police. I asked him down to talk about security," Koren said quickly.

"But George looks after security." She pointed at the bursar. "Don't you, George?" Here was some entertainment, her expression said.

"I thought I did. It *was* my responsibility."

"It's the president's responsibility ultimately, George," Koren said. "I know the security guards report to you, but that's just an administrative convenience because we don't have a V.P. Admin. They could just as easily report to Tommy. I'm following up an initiative of Dr. Mackane's. Revising our needs."

"But you're not the president!" Esther Kleinburg cried. "Is he?" She addressed the table at large. "You're just the acting president, aren't you?"

It was so rude that Salter wondered if Koren might throw his soup over her, but when nothing happened and the poet went back to her macaroni, shaking her head and smiling, he wondered if she was mad.

The young instructor with a fringe of beard spoke up. He had been watching the eminent scholar with a look of devoted interest, and now he had a remark ready. "The Literary Society has asked me to be the faculty adviser on the *Vanbrugh Review*." He chuckled. "I declined on the grounds that the term 'adviser' is clearly a euphemism for censor and suggested they find someone who teaches comparative religion." He waited for an answering smile.

The eminent scholar finished his macaroni. "I was the faculty adviser last year. If anyone had called me the censor I'd have told him to stick the review up his arse." He leaned back to accept the pastry and applesauce over his shoulder.

Everyone except the young instructor laughed—a bit heartily, Salter thought—and the conversation became general.

They returned to the common room for coffee, after which Orchard went off to look for Mackane's appointment book and Salter went back with Koren to his office.

"What was going on at lunch?" Salter asked.

"Oh, Timbrell deserved it. Burns is a kind man, but Timbrell is always sucking up to him and the old boy just got bored with him."

"I meant the stuff about the president. She was getting at you, wasn't she?"

"They all were. But that's college politics, of no interest to you. Has Orchard been helpful? I don't want to know the details."

"He's told me everything I needed to know."

"Good. He's a remarkable fellow. Completely uneducated, of course. Got to high table on sheer ability."

"He can read and write, can't he?"

"Of course. I meant a man in his position would normally have a business diploma or some such so that he wouldn't feel out of place. He came here as a storekeeper, I think, before my time. When his supervisor quit, Orchard quite rightly was given the job. He's demonstrated the most extraordinary knack for getting things done. He looks after everything—the homecoming parades, convocation—everything like that, and he's wonderful at getting people in town to lend us things. But he must feel out of place sometimes. He told you what you wanted to know, did he?"

Salter nodded. How many more times are you going to ask me? he wondered.

They were interrupted by Orchard, who appeared in the doorway with Mackane's appointment book in his hand.

Salter took the book from him and turned to shake hands with Koren, thanking him for his help, and for lunch, making a ceremony of it and ending by accompanying Orchard back to his own office.

"Here you are," Orchard said. He handed Salter a large envelope and helped him put in the book and the picture.

He was finished with Orchard now, but after the cut-and-thrust atmosphere of lunch he was inclined to rest for a few minutes in the company of the diffident supervisor. "You must miss Dr. Mackane," he said, stretching out his legs and laying the envelope aside.

"Very much. This is a good billet under him. I'll get used to the change, though. You always do."

"You were in the Army," Salter said.

"The British Army. For three years."

Some trace of it remained in the heavy, brown, highly polished shoes, in the neat look of the striped tie sitting in the center of the white shirt. Orchard had the habit of neatness, of squaring off his corners to pass inspection, a habit Salter shared, picked up in his uniformed days.

"When did you come out here?"

"Seventy-four."

"Straight to Marlborough?"

"More or less. I had a couple of jobs first, but they weren't much of an improvement over what I'd left behind in England. Then I saw an ad for this place and I've been here ever since."

"You like that gang I saw at lunch?"

"I know what you're saying. But I'm outside all that. They are all very decent to me."

"Who's going to take over, do you think? Koren?"

"I understand the Board of Governors is searching for a new president and he has applied."

"You hope he gets it?"

Orchard looked at the door. "No, I don't." He made several brisk movements, indicating his desire to change the subject.

Salter took the hint. He had thought that Orchard might welcome a few minutes away from the officers' mess, as it were, but the man clearly did not want to let his hair down with Salter. His attitude said that it was no business of the inspector's. Salter stood up and put out his hand. "Good luck, Mr. Orchard. I hope everything goes well."

"I'm sure it will." He gave Salter's hand a single shake. "I don't suppose you will need to come back. After all, Dr. Mackane has been in hospital for a month, and this lady was killed last week. It obviously has nothing to do with him. I don't know why their relationship should concern you at all."

"In this work you often don't know yourself. You have to ask about everything. Nine tenths of it is a waste of time." Now it was Salter's turn to appear dismissive. "You've done your bit," he said, looking at his watch. "Now I need a washroom."

"On your left," Orchard said, and Salter disappeared down the corridor.

DRIVING HOME through the prespring landscape, brown after the winter runoff, Salter allowed the day's events to drift through his brain without trying to order them. Orchard had left him feeling uncomfortable. The man clearly did not own his position; he had kept it largely by teaching Mackane tennis and maybe by arranging his alibi when Mackane wanted to see Linda Thomas. If Koren got to be president, Orchard would be back in the servants' quarters, the sergeants' mess, whatever that was on a college campus. Salter felt sorry for him, for there was nothing dislikable about the man. He hoped Orchard would not fall too far.

He tried to think. He tried the trick of writing a report in his head. The report would confine itself to the fact that Mackane could be crossed off the list. Orchard had confirmed everything the psychotherapist, Sheila Barnsley, had already told him, that Dr. Mackane was the secret lover, and the entry in her appointment book meant only that Linda Thomas was planning to see him every other Friday, and she had filled in all their meeting times in a rush of love at the beginning of the year.

There were two problems. The first was how and when Linda Thomas had learned of Mackane's collapse. This was not impossible to answer. Salter imagined her waiting on the Friday afternoon a month before for the lover who was never to come again, waiting perhaps two more weeks for a second disappointment, then realizing something must have happened when he did not even call. Finally, needing to know—assuming a false identity, perhaps—telephoning Marlborough and learning what she feared, then having to nurse her misery in silence and alone. Sheila Barnsley had said nothing about her acting strangely in the month before her death, so evidently Linda

Thomas had retained a powerful hold on her emotions.

The second problem was more difficult. If Mackane was not the man who had shared her wine that afternoon, who was? Could she have acquired another lover so quickly? It made no sense of the character Salter had learned about, a woman whose fidelity would surely last for a long time after Mackane's death. But someone had had sex with her that afternoon.

He parked his car, realizing that he had hardly thought about his own troubles all day, but that ended when he returned to the office and was met by the staff psychologist, who wanted to discuss with him the statistics on failed marriages among policemen. And there was a message from Annie saying that she was going to be working late and would not be home for dinner. The message filled him with relief and anxiety. Relief because he had not yet done anything about their trip; anxiety because he wondered if he drove past her office when he left, would he find it closed and everyone gone? Some of the anxiety dissipated when she called to see if he had gotten her message and to say she really was working late and he could call her at the office during the evening if there was any problem at home. Not all of it, though, because she added that it might be a long evening and not to wait up for her. So they would have to wait another day to move into the next stage.

ELEVEN

PICKETT LISTENED as Salter ran through the events at Marlborough. "So we're still looking for the guy she was drinking with that afternoon," Salter concluded.

"Or woman."

"You think that's likely?"

"No, I don't, but I didn't think it wouldn't be Mackane, either."

"Any luck with the block?"

"Nothing real. That woman I told you about, the one who claimed to know nothing, says she doesn't even know what the janitor looks like, which is pretty weird. She's lived there for eight years."

"Did you find anyone who shared the opinion of the janitor's wife? That she was on the game?"

"No one. She was a therapist and a typist. One of the old ladies ran across her in Grand and Toy, buying stationery."

"So what's with the janitor's wife?"

"They all think she's jealous of her old man. It's the joke of the block. Whenever he had any repairs in any of the apartments of the single women, she would usually come by with a message, making sure he wasn't jumping the tenants while he was fixing the radiators."

"That likely?"

"Not while she was around. He had plenty of opportunities in the daytime, though. I wondered about that. Could be that the woman who won't talk to me has been warned off by the wife. Maybe she came home once and caught Turnow coming out of her apartment when he should have been stoking the furnace."

Salter grunted. "We're going to have to start again. Call the television guy. Ask him if Linda Thomas seemed upset in the past month." He looked around his desk. "What else?" he wondered aloud.

"You could go through her appointment book again. Maybe talk to her minister. She belonged to the Anglican church the Welsh go to in Toronto. Taffy Williams, the supervisor in Bail and Parole, told me. He's an altar boy or some such in the same church."

"Welsh Anglicans? In Toronto?"

"You name it, we've got it. I investigated a complaint in Scarborough once, when there still were fields out there. A farmer complaining about someone having a party in one of his fields one night. It turned out to be a bunch of Latvian tree-worshipers celebrating midnight Mass."

Salter, barely listening, said, "Call the deputy minister, too. Same question: Was Thomas upset lately?"

"Do that yourself," Pickett urged. "He's pissed off with me. Let him think you've taken me off the case. He may respond without a lot of bullshit. I told you, I think there's something funny going on with him."

"He's got a solid alibi."

"Yeah. Suspicious, isn't it?"

"Maybe you're right. I'll go and talk to him." Salter made a note on a pad. Pickett stood up. "By the way, Mel, that girl was in again," Salter said as Pickett reached the door.

"Who?"

"That kid looking for her relative. Had any thoughts?"

Pickett turned away, shaking his head. Salter stopped him in the doorway. "She says the guy was in the Air Force, stationed in Bournemouth, in England, during the war. Ring any bells?"

"Be retired now, if he ever joined the police in the first place. No."

"I guess. She's coming back tomorrow, at ten. Would you talk to her? See if she tells you anything that might help to locate him?"

"I'd just as soon not. I've got a lot on my plate. Besides, what could I tell her that you don't know?"

"If she hears it from you, someone who's been around as long as you have, maybe she'll go away. She's a hell of a persistent character. Come in for a few minutes, eh? At ten. In the office here."

It was an order. Pickett looked at Salter for a long time, gathering the message, then shrugged. "Whatever you say, sir."

IN HIS OFFICE, edgy, the girl on his mind, Pickett dialed the number of Doughty, the television host.

Anything to keep busy. "Mr. Doughty? One question: When did you last see Miss Thomas?"

"A week before she died."

"And before that?"

"Three weeks, I think. Then five. It's all in her appointment book, surely?"

"We're learning not to trust that book."

"You mean someone could've substituted a phony appointment book? Deleting himself? What a fantastic idea! That's terrific!"

"For that book you're writing, maybe. All I'm concerned with is a couple of canceled appointments we want to check out. No mastermind. Let me ask you one more question. Did she seem upset to you at any time? Especially during the past month. Did she seem bothered by anything?"

"Not that I noticed. She was always a very calm person. I'd tell her jokes and she'd have a little laugh, or I'd tell her what a hell of a time I was having at work and she'd sympathize a little. Not much reaction either way. She was a pro, kept herself out of her work, like a doctor. Why? Are you closing in?"

"Or just pissing about. I'm not sure."

"You mind if I stay in touch?"

"I'd like you to, especially if you can remember anything she told you about her personal life."

"I meant, you know, to hear how it works out, how you solve it. This is *interesting*."

"Yeah? Right now all I can tell you is we've got a number of leads."

Doughty laughed. "Nobody helping you with your inquiries?"

"Lots of people. You, for instance."

"I mean, you haven't got anyone in a back room somewhere."

"We call that 'held for questioning.' No."

"Now can I ask *you* a couple of questions?"

"What about?"

"I'd like to know what someone like you does when you're off-duty. Do you socialize with other policemen? What kind of assignments do you like most? Are there any kind you hate? And I need some jargon. Street talk. Do you use words like 'stoolie'? And what holidays do you get? All kinds of stuff for color. Could I come to your office or home?"

"Mr. Doughty, right now I've got a lot on my mind. People like you who want professional assistance are supposed to go through the chief. I'll have to talk to my boss. Why don't I get someone to give you a ride round in a squad car. That's what writers generally do."

"Could you fix that?"

"I'll speak to one of the people I know. Give me a few days. Look, I'll fix it up on my own, but keep it to yourself, will you? We've had a lot of guys like you lately."

"Terrific. I'll wait until I hear from you."

MEANWHILE, SALTER WAS telephoning Curry, the deputy minister. He gave Curry's secretary his name and was connected immediately. They exchanged no greetings. Curry said, "I have nothing more to tell you. I told that sergeant I don't want to hear from you again. Is that clear?"

"We need your help," Salter said. "And telephones are not a good way of keeping stuff private. Can I come and see you? I'd be very grateful. Or would you prefer to come down here?"

There was a long pause while Curry thought about the last question. "One more time, then," he said. "Be here in twenty minutes."

THIS TIME THERE WAS no hanging around in outer offices. Curry waited for Salter to close the door and looked at his watch. "What is it?" he asked as Salter was still standing.

Salter sat down and checked his own watch. "I want to verify every appointment she made," he began. "We can't establish who was with her that afternoon. She had a phony name in her book."

"And this is what you wanted to know? What will satisfy you? Perhaps this." He held out a hand flat as Salter began to protest, and picked up the phone. "Miss Jennings, bring in the letter from Mr. Lestrode, will you?"

Once more Salter tried to speak, but Curry waved him quiet. The secretary came through the door with a sheet of paper in her hand. Curry took it from her and snapped it straight. "Don't go away, Miss Jennings. We need you."

The woman stood still, looking frightened. Salter sat back as Curry began to read.

"It is from J. Lestrode, my counterpart in Ottawa. Dated Tuesday. 'Dear Nick: Further to our meeting here on April 14, I would like to confirm that the policy we discussed is undergoing review. At the moment, in order for you to qualify for federal funds...'" Curry broke off. "The rest is confidential, Inspector, even from you. Let me just read the ending. 'I enjoyed our chat and the minister was glad of the chance to meet you himself. Yours, Jim.' Ottawa, Inspector. The federal deputy *and* the minister. Now, Miss Jennings: Tell us what travel arrangements you made for me that day."

"The usual ones, sir, first class return on the train. Leaving Toronto on Thursday night. Leaving Ottawa at one-twenty the next day."

"Why are those my usual travel arrangements when I go to Ottawa?"

"I beg your pardon, sir?"

"Why do I go by train? Tell him."

"Because you don't like flying, and you like to work on the train. Is that right?"

"That's right. You can go now." He turned to Salter. "Now, Inspector. Call Ottawa. Confirm that I was there, then get out of my life. That clear?"

Salter was now as angry as Curry, but he had more experience at not showing it. "I don't know what that was all about, sir," he allowed himself to say, testing his own poise. "It had nothing to do with what I want to know. We were satisfied the first time you told us. What I want to know is something else entirely."

After some seconds, Curry twitched his head, a tiny flick, and Salter went on. "We've come across some discrepancies in her appointment book, and they add up to a question. We think she might have been very upset about a month ago. Did you notice anything depressed or disturbed about her at that time?"

"And *that's* what you're bothering me with?"

"It might be important. Right now, it's a puzzle."

"Then, no. I did not notice anything depressed or disturbed about her at that time, or at any other time. Or that she was happy or well balanced, either. We didn't chat. She massaged me. Is that it?"

"That's it."

"Were you hoping for a different answer?"

"Just the right one."

"In that case, for Christ's sake don't bother me again." Curry turned his attention to a file on his desk.

Salter stood up. "Does your secretary know what I am?"

Curry spoke into his file. "Of course she does. But she doesn't know why you're here. I'll tell her you are investigating the travel expenses of senior civil servants, shall I?"

"That should satisfy her. I imagine that happens."

On the way back Salter daydreamed the impossible dream of blowing a hole through Curry's story. He needed a fantasy to channel his fury. And then, running through the conversation in his head, inventing new crushing replies for himself, he heard Curry again, spelling out his travel arrangements. Why? With a deputy minister in Ottawa backing up his story at one end and his wife at the other, why did his travel arrangements matter? A great deal, apparently. He tucked the question away, to be picked at when he had run out of things to do.

JENNY SCHUMANN was waiting for him in her antiques store on Yorkville. When he arrived she put on her coat immediately and they walked down to the cafe in Hazelton Lanes. She was a tall, attractively graying woman in her fifties who wore a lot of gold jewelry, this time over a red dress encrusted around the neck with rhinestones and gold wire. Heads turned when they entered the restaurant and when the waiter helped her off with her coat. She was obviously somebody.

She had originally been Annie's friend who had become Salter's, and he had confided in her before, in a limited way. She affected to lust after Salter and often warned Annie she would take him off her hands. Annie understood that Jenny's noisy declaration of her interest in Salter was her way of protecting herself from doing anything about her real interest. The two women were close friends, as were Salter and Jenny, so, curiously, she had become a way for Salter to talk about his home life without being disloyal to Annie. After their lunch, he knew, she might call Annie and tell her what happened, though perhaps not all.

Salter started right in: "Annie's been seeing some guy."

She reached out a lean, enamel-tipped hand for a piece of bread, broke it in pieces, and started chewing.

"She's not having an affair," he continued. Then he told her the story. "So we're going to Italy," he concluded.

"That's all right, then. Just Italian lessons. Why are you telling me? I mean, why did I have to get my assistant in an hour early so we could have lunch?"

"You heard. What am I doing wrong? See, I thought she might be having an affair. But she isn't. But I'm still not sure what it's all about."

"You're not?" She leaned back to let the waiter serve her, then sipped her wine. When they were both eating, she began, in short, hard sentences, spoken between bites of her fish.

"So she isn't having a little fling that she might get over." She chewed and swallowed. "Not a little romance." Another pause, and she pushed her plate away. "Don't look like that, Charlie. I know you. For you, Annie in bed with someone else would be shattering news, but it might just mean she's joined the human race—the one I live in, anyway. I'd be surprised, and you'd have to do some adjusting. But this is different."

"I couldn't believe she was sleeping with some guy."

"She wasn't. She was just enjoying his company, enjoying talking to him. Enough so she didn't tell me about it." She lit a cigarette and watched him think.

"It's worse, isn't it? That's what I've been afraid of."

"Worse than what? Than what you thought? Yes, I think it is."

"What'll I do?"

"Something, that's for sure. Don't give up. But you're going to have to do something."

"What?"

"To start with, look at your life from her point of view. Angus is gone. When he comes back from Europe he'll be off to university. Seth will be around for another, what? Three or four years? Then what? There's a name for it. I know Annie's not interested in keeping that job much longer. It got her out of her last rut, but it isn't what she wants to do with her life. But if she quits, what's she got to face? You won't retire for another ten years, maybe. You're back in the saddle again. So when the kids are gone, what's she going to do? Go back to being a housewife, waiting for you to come home for dinner?"

"A lot of women do it."

"A lot of policemen's marriages break up, too."

"I could retire now. With my pension and her money, we'd be all right. Oh, shit no, I'm not going to quit."

"Don't thrash around. What would you do if you did retire? Play golf while she looks after the house? I think she may be seeing that in her future, and it frightens her."

"Have you been talking to her?"

"Not yet, but I don't have to. We talk a lot. You're a cranky bastard, Charlie Salter. You've had your ups and downs and you've said more than once, when things got rough, that you might quit. That would have been interesting news to her ten years ago, but now it's scary. She wants a life after retirement."

"It'd be different then."

"Not if you don't start now. Annie's right: You're egocentric."

"She called me a pig."

"That'll do. I don't doubt you act like one when you don't want to do something, which, according to her, is most of the time. Maybe you should separate. How important is she to you?" She watched him react with contempt for the question. "All right. Then do something."

"What? What?"

"Don't ask me. This isn't a one-shot thing, like buying her a fur coat. You've got to start thinking about her again."

"It sounds to me like you're saying I have to start courting her again."

She burst into laughter and leaned over and kissed him. "What a gorgeous word, and it'll do for a start. You had fun when you were courting her, didn't you? And in the early days, before the kids arrived."

"Oh, yeah. It was great."

"So think your way back to it. Try having an affair yourself. With Annie."

He was still troubled. "But there's a lot of stuff she likes I can't do."

Then Jenny was tired. The coffee came and she started to organize herself. "I've given it my best shot, Charlie. You'll have to go to work on it. Start with Italy. And remember, if you do break up, I'll take you on."

"Yes, until you realize I'm not interested in antiques, either." He picked up the bill. "Can I ask you one more favor? Don't tell Annie."

"That's a problem. I don't want any secrets. What'll I do if someone tells her they saw us in here today? You tell her, please."

"No, no. Not that. She knows we talk. I mean just about courting."

She laughed again. "Okay, that was your word. I'll just tell her we had lunch and I'm on her side."

HE WALKED toward Yonge Street, thinking hard. Roses, he thought. Then, no. Roses is a knee-jerk gesture, like a fur coat. What, then? Italy first. He bought a map of Europe and returned to his office. First he blocked off the whole of June and the first week of July. Four weeks for Italy and one for golf and fishing. Then he stared at the map of Europe for half an hour, long enough to generate an active response. He started to put crosses on some of the places he had read about. Then he phoned Air France and gave them his order, arranging to have the whole thing delivered to his office by courier. Then, after all, he phoned a florist.

THAT NIGHT AT DINNER they said nothing until Seth was out of the way. The only sign of anything amiss now was that she had gone to some trouble to pick up a loaf of good bread to go with the pasta, and made a more elaborate salad than usual.

After dinner, in the living room, he began producing little packages. "One," he said: "Return ticket to Paris. A month. Two: I've bought a Renault, which we sell them back at the end. Three: A map of Europe. See the crosses? Those are the places I want to see. Paris, Venice, Monte Carlo. You fill in your crosses and we'll draw the route. Let's spend a week in Tuscany." He took a deep breath. "When you see your friend next, ask him what's the best way to stay in Tuscany for a week. We could go back to Florence or to that place with the wall 'round it."

"We could get a villa."

"Whatever. When you've decided, I'll buy some guidebooks."

"No, I'll do that. I want...no, sorry, *you* buy some guidebooks, okay. I'd like to stay in a hotel in Switzerland for at least one night. I'll ask Marjorie about villas. She knows all about how to rent them." She gathered up the packages and brought her knees together. "I can't ask Giuseppe. Something happened today. I wrote to him thanking him for all his help and told him I wouldn't be seeing him anymore.''

"What happened? You mean something *happened,* or just you were thinking about this thing.'' He waited, and when she didn't speak, he said, "I don't mind if you see the guy.''

She shook her head. "He sent me some roses today. To the office. I was afraid he would do something like this, and when I got them I got a bit frightened and I decided I couldn't have that.''

"How did he sign them? Love and kisses, something like that?''

"Not quite.''

Salter sipped at the remains of his coffee. "It wasn't him, it was me. I'll tell you what it said: 'From an Admirer,' right? I wasn't trying to be funny—well, maybe I was, in case anyone in your office read the card. I didn't want to say it on a card. But I do love you.''

She looked up, distraught and appalled. "Oh, Jesus, I'm sorry.'' Then she was crying. "I *know* you do.''

Her assumption, and its implications, shook slightly the bridge they had thrown up between them in the past two evenings, but for now he was happy with the result. "That's enough. Let's walk down to Lichtman's and look at guidebooks. Both of us. We've got ten minutes to get out of here before Seth gets back.''

It would register very high on the Richter scale: There were cracks in the walls and rubble all over the place. But the foundations were still in place, surely to God.

AS IF PICKETT DIDN'T HAVE enough to worry about, he got home that night to find his sister-in-law and nephew waiting in her car outside his house. If he had had his wits about him he would have recognized the car and tried to avoid them, but they saw him and she waved and he pulled in behind them. He let them in the house and Willis, delighted at the prospect of company, tried to romp with Verna, who recoiled as if the dog were a rat. Willis moved on to Pickett's nephew, Harvey, who playfully put a boot on Willis's back and pressed him into the rug, sending the dog into a frenzy.

"Leave her alone!" Pickett ordered. The nephew lifted his boot and Willis shot across the room and fenced himself in behind Pickett's feet.

"Why don't you get rid of it?" Verna suggested, settling her face into an agreeable expression. "I know you only got it for Mary. You never really liked it, did you? I don't blame you. Give it away. Sell it."

"It's a 'she,'" Pickett said.

"Willis? Sounds like a 'he,' doesn't it? I always forget."

"It's a 'she.'"

"Anyway, you don't have to keep it, just because of me."

It took Pickett a minute to sort out the implications of what she was saying, her assumption that he was keeping the dog because he thought she, Verna, might be offended if he got rid of it, it being Mary's dog, but in fact she (Verna) would understand if he now took the opportunity to get rid of it. She was being gracious. How could he demonstrate that he didn't give a pinch of coonshit what she thought?

She was a narrow woman, a few years younger than he, married to a roofer in Hamilton. Their one son was a lout of twenty who had already had half a dozen dead-end jobs since dropping out of school in grade ten. Pickett would have been happy to let the connection fade; he disliked the blade-faced Verna as much as he disliked anyone, but she was determined to keep him in the family. Pickett ate turkey twice a year in Hamilton and Verna called on him once a month, usually with Harvey in tow, ostensibly making the sixty-mile trip for other reasons but always finding time to make sure Pickett was still all right. When Harvey acquired a motorcycle he occasionally appeared on his own, sitting in Pickett's kitchen for fifteen minutes with nothing to say beyond what the traffic had been like on the Gardiner Expressway. About a year before, Verna had told Pickett that Harvey would like to join the police, like his uncle, and asked him to help get the boy in. But Pickett was much more a policeman than he was Harvey's uncle, and he had made sure the application was rejected. The incident explained to him why Verna kept up the connection in the face of his inertia: She had always seen Pickett as someone who might get the boy started in life, her own husband being useless in this regard. But when, after Harvey had failed to get into the police, she continued to call, he realized that her vision was larger than the immediate future. A comment from her about the rise of real-estate values in Toronto put him on the right track: In the absence of blood relatives, Harvey was Pickett's assumed heir, and Pickett's house and any savings bonds he had tucked away were being earmarked by her for the boy's future. Pickett was in excellent health, but men of his age often died suddenly, she knew, especially after they retired, and she was keeping Harvey properly positioned to be his natural beneficiary. The turkey dinners in Hamilton at Thanksgiving and Christmas were designed to create a debt of gratitude; the visits to Toronto were to keep an eye on him. Pickett had solid confirmation of all this when they called unexpectedly one Sunday afternoon and found him drinking a beer in the librarian's garden after he had finished cutting the grass. He returned to his house to endure the visit and found himself being cross-examined about the librarian and finally (Verna could not restrain herself) being warned against her and her kind. Pickett should not be fooled, Verna said. Lots of women would see him as a nice meal ticket. She'd seen plenty of that in Hamilton. Her thin face quivered with earnestness as she kept her eyes on him, waiting for some sign that she could relax.

Pickett was so angry with her, on his own behalf, on behalf of the librarian, and at the way in which, as he put it to himself, his sister-in-law was pissing all over one of the nicest relationships he had ever had, that he said nothing at all, which she took as some indication that all her wisdom was filling his head, and she returned to Hamilton satisfied. Pickett made a resolution to see a lawyer the next day and make a will to leave everything he had to the librarian, and then, realizing that if he dropped dead a week later, such a will would only embarrass the lady, he searched for alternatives, entertaining briefly half a dozen different charities.

In the end, he did nothing, of course. The next day he still liked the idea, but he put off calling a lawyer. He was busy, for one thing, but something else prevented him. He was not quite up to the audacity of wiping out all Verna's expectations with a single sentence, and some echo from the grave, a ghostly hand laid on his arm, reminded him that Harvey was his wife's nephew, too.

Pickett rubbed the dog's back. "What brings you here?"

"Taking a course," the boy said.

Pickett waited for more.

Verna spoke up. "He's going to get his certificate. In welding. He can do it as well as anybody in the garage, but he doesn't have a certificate for the big jobs. He's going to do a course here. Which college is it, Harvey?"

"Kenzie."

"Mackenzie College. It's run by the government."

While he waited to find out what all this had to do with him, Pickett lifted Willis onto his lap, where she licked any of his fingers that came within reach.

"He needs a place to stay," Verna said.

Pickett took two fingers out of the dog's mouth. "Does he now?"

"We thought you might be able to help out."

"I could ask around. I've seen ads in the laundromat. Would he want board and room?"

"We thought you could find room for him here."

Pickett seemed to give this some consideration as a new idea, deserving respect. Why can't I just tell her I'd sooner keep a baboon in the basement? he wondered. He knew the answer as the face of his dead wife surfaced, pleading with him to keep the peace. "You can see the way it is here," he said eventually. "There's just this room and the kitchen and bathroom where the dining room used to be. I've got my bed in the basement. Where would I put him?"

"Upstairs, we thought."

It took his breath away, although he ought to have been ready for it. She was seriously proposing that he take in Harvey as his tenant. Rent-free, probably.

"There are people living upstairs."

"Harvey's course doesn't start until the first of May."

"You think I could give these people notice?" He couldn't believe it.

"Harvey *is* your nephew. He was always Mary's favorite."

Once more Pickett searched for the way to tell her; once more he chickened out. "The two I've got now are students. I can't upset them like that in the middle of their exams."

"When do they finish? Are they at the university? They're all finished in May. Harvey could manage for a week or two on the couch here, couldn't you, Harvey?"

"Yeah."

"There's the Landlord and Tenants Act. I'm not allowed to kick them out."

"You could ask them. If they are students they are probably going anyway. They won't mind going a few days sooner."

In fact, the tenants had already told Pickett they were leaving early in May, to go to work at a holiday lodge in northern Ontario. "They graduate this year, so they may stay on. Get jobs in the city. I'll ask them."

"When could you let Harvey know?"

"Next week?" That ought to be time enough to create an impenetrable lie, or to get up the nerve to tell her to stuff it.

"We'll come down on Wednesday, then."

Harvey leaned forward and poked Willis in the face with his finger, setting the dog barking furiously. Verna's face twisted in irritation. "Why don't you put it outside while we're talking?"

"She doesn't like it outside. Besides, I thought we'd finished."

"Aren't you going to offer us a cup of coffee?"

"Rather have a beer," Harvey said.

On it went for another hour while Pickett made coffee, found two bottles of beer for Harvey, and Verna kept up a stream of chat about the life and times of the family in Hamilton, endless narratives that Pickett tuned out while he wrestled with his anxieties. Finally the two of them left, but even as they were in the hall, Pickett's tenants arrived home and Verna's face lit up and she turned to him, registering that this was the perfect opportunity for him to settle it then and there, and Pickett was obliged to thrust Harvey through the door and his mother after him before she could raise the question. He squeezed Willis to make her bark and appeared to struggle with the dog, making it necessary to close the door in her face.

TWELVE

PICKETT WOKE UP very early the next morning, before dawn. He was used to that. The problem with age, he had discovered, is keeping a normal rhythm in the day. If he lived naturally, he would be in bed at eight-thirty and up at four every day. If he slept for an hour after supper he would lie awake until two o'clock in the morning. What he really needed was an hour's sleep after lunch, a hard thing to arrange in the Bail and Parole Unit. This morning he was disturbed by a teeming brain that had finally fought off the effects of the six ounces of scotch he had drunk to put himself to sleep. The major anxiety was Harvey, his nephew, but the girl was there, too, waiting for him to make up his mind what to do about her.

Through the small basement window he saw a hint of dawn leaching through the clear night sky. He waited, trying to doze, until it was full daylight, but when he got up, finally, he still had several hours to fill in before his meeting with the girl. For the time it took him to find his slippers and bathrobe, he let himself be distracted by her. He wondered briefly if the staff inspector were playing some game, for he had to have come across the possibility that Pickett was the man the girl was looking for.

Willis was waiting to lick him into life from the top of the basement stairs, and Pickett got the dog some food while his coffee dripped through. After he had showered, it was time to take the dog for a walk and pick up a newspaper. Gradually the hours wore away, and he left the house with just enough time before the meeting.

HE KEPT HIS DOOR OPEN slightly so he could hear the girl arrive, and he tried to think about the case of the strangled masseuse. At five minutes to the hour he heard Salter greet the girl, and he took himself off to the washroom. A three-minute wait there, spent mainly in trying to see what he looked like in the mirror, and he charged out and into Salter's office, where the girl was waiting, watching the door. Salter was pretending to catch up on his paperwork.

"This is the young lady I was telling you about, Mel. This is Sergeant Pickett, Miss Colwood."

Pickett sat down and made himself look at her calmly. His first sight of her had made no sense, and he had looked around the office to see if there was another girl. She was dressed entirely in black cotton. Her hair was arranged in blue and silver spikes, and her eyes were surrounded by circles of blue paint. A large silver dot adorned one cheekbone.

"What can I do for you?" Pickett waited for the snarl or whine that her appearance seemed bound to produce. This, he thought, has nothing to do with me.

"It's very kind of you to take so much trouble." Her voice was low and soft, and her accent was the kind Pickett associated with heroines of British plays on television. "Staff Inspector Salter suggested that if I told you what I know about my relative it might jog your memory. My relative must have been a colleague of yours, he thinks."

The clownish costume had drained away and Pickett heard only the voice and saw the face of Olive Colwood, reincarnated after forty years. He felt frightened, slightly out of control. When he tried a relaxed gesture, crossing his legs, he was so rigid that he had to force his body to rearrange itself.

"What do you know about him?"

She began by repeating what Salter had already told him. The man she was looking for had been stationed in England, in Bournemouth, in 1945 in the Canadian Air Force. There she stopped.

Pickett looked at Salter, and the staff inspector stood up. "I've got someone coming in a few minutes. Take Miss Colwood into your office, would you, Mel?" He turned to the girl. "You know, miss, if we do find the man you're looking for, if Sergeant Pickett comes up with a name, we aren't obliged to tell you."

"I know. He may not want to meet me. I've thought of that. But I'd like to give him a message."

"You could write it down and we'll pass it on, if we know who to send it to. But if he doesn't want to reply..." Salter shrugged.

"Then I won't bother him anymore. But I would like to give him a message."

Salter nodded and waited for them to leave.

IN HIS OWN OFFICE, Pickett floundered on. "How do you know this guy is or was in the police?"

"He came over to England once or twice in the fifties and got in touch with my grandmother."

Pickett tried to think of the questions an ignorant outsider would ask, but there was no way of avoiding it: All questions led to the ones he wanted to avoid.

"In what way is this man related to you?"

"He was connected to my grandmother."

"Brother? Cousin? What?" Make her say it, he thought.

"Could you promise me this is in confidence?"

"Why?"

"I don't want to cause embarrassment."

"If it's that personal, maybe you should forget the whole thing."

"I would like to see him, to meet him, if it's possible."

"Why? You don't know anything about him."

"Yes, I do. My grandmother said he was the most wonderful man she had ever known."

Pickett knew then that he was destroyed. "All right, this is between us, I promise you. What else?"

"Thank you. I asked Inspector Salter about you. He said I could trust you."

Did he? What does he know? he thought. "So how are you related?"

"He's my grandfather."

The relief at the thing said was very great, as if Pickett himself had confessed. "Better tell me it all," he said.

"My grandmother was in the WAAF during the war. She became pregnant, and one of the Canadians on the station admitted he was the father. But he refused to marry her and then went back to Canada."

"That doesn't sound too wonderful. But he's been back?"

"Yes, twice at least. A long time ago, before I was born. He managed to find her, and that's how she knew he was in the police."

"Did she tell you all this?" Where is she now? he wondered. And then he had a premonition, or something of the kind, a sense that the girl had been sent to feel him out, that Olive Colwood was in Toronto, looking for him. Wouldn't that be something, he thought. "Where is she now?" he asked, meaning, Which hotel?

"She died a little while ago, just before Christmas. That's when I heard the story. My father told me after the funeral."

"Didn't you ever ask about your grandfather?"

"I understood he had died during the war, but my father told me after the funeral that he just disappeared. So my father was illegitimate. He never meant to tell me. There was all that 'turn Annie's face to the wall' kind of thing with him. All I know is that my grandmother insisted he was wonderful but he wouldn't marry her. Then, after the funeral, we found this picture.'' She opened a kind of leather sack she was carrying and brought out a wallet, a huge thing with a thong around it suitable for carrying pieces of bread and meat on pilgrimages. The picture she produced was of a young couple in Air Force uniform leaning against the rail of a seafront promenade. ''We think that must be him.''

''That's not him,'' Pickett said immediately.

The girl looked at the picture, then at Pickett, then again at the picture, and finally returned to Pickett's face for a long time. ''I think it must be. It's the only picture from those days she kept.''

''That's not him. I don't know why she would keep that picture. That's Billy Crow. He was just one of the gang.''

''I see.'' Slowly the girl returned the picture to her wallet, wrapped the thong around it, and returned the wallet to her sack. Then she waited.

Pickett said, ''You'd better come to the house tonight.'' He wrote the address on the back of a card. ''I'll be home by six. Take the Yonge Street subway to St. Clair. Then a streetcar west to Humewood Gardens.''

The girl held the card out and away from her, as if it were about to catch fire. ''You are my grandmother's friend?''

"I'm the guy you're looking for, yes. Come to the house tonight and we'll get caught up. I don't know about what, though. There's not much to say."

The girl stood up. "Would you thank Inspector Salter for me? He was very helpful."

Yes, and I wonder why? Pickett thought. "I'll do that." He shepherded her though the door and almost out of the building, trying to decide what to do about Salter. He bumped into the staff inspector on his way back to his office and postponed the problem. "I think I can help her," he said. "I'll let you know."

Salter nodded, apparently not interested. "Know of someone, do you?" he said and turned away.

PICKETT BADLY NEEDED time to consider and decide how to handle the girl, himself, and Salter. Always in front of his mind he had the absolute knowledge that he could simply retire, which would take care of Salter and the rest of them, but he still had to decide how to deal with the girl, and unpick his emotions concerning her. Once he had confirmed that, the problem of Salter shrank, and he found he was able to contemplate telling Salter the truth without telling him why he hadn't told him it immediately. Fuck him. Now for the girl. Her ridiculous appearance had long faded, been gotten used to, and been replaced by the general impression of what a nice kid she was. He was just deciding that he wanted to be agreeable to her, if she would let him, when he was interrupted by Salter, looking concerned.

"I've had a call from the chief. The deputy minister is raising the roof."

"What did you do to him?"

"Nothing. I'd just about crossed him off the list, but he said he's going to call on the Ontario Provincial Police to investigate what he calls our totally illegal surveillance of his private life."

"What the hell is he on about?" This was better than thinking about the girl.

"I don't have the faintest idea. All I did was talk to him in his office. There's no surveillance, for Christ's sake. Interesting, though, isn't it? What he thinks, I mean."

"Maybe you should see him again. Find out what he's talking about. I'll go if you like. I'll take full responsibility for all aspects of the investigation involving Mr. Curry." Pickett squared his shoulders as if for news photographers. All this was a great diversion.

Salter laughed. "You want to tangle with him, don't you? Tell him to go fuck himself, on camera, then come back here and resign. No way. I'll go see Curry."

"Too bad. I've still got to show those pictures around the block. You'd better call his office first, just in case he won't speak to you."

Salter left and returned almost immediately. "He's waiting for me. I think he's looking forward to reaming me out. From his point of view I should be pissing my pants."

WHEN HE ARRIVED at the deputy minister's office, Curry motioned him to a seat, hunched himself in the back of his own chair, and said, "I agreed to see you because I thought you should have a chance to explain yourself before I nailed your balls to my desk."

"Yes? What about, sir?"

"All right. I'll go through the farce. About this gorilla you had on my tail."

"Gorilla on your tail?"

"The man you've got following me in a blue car. A Plymouth. A copper in plain clothes."

"Have you perhaps been involved in any other activities that could account for this? Could he be a bailiff? A debt collector?"

"You smart sonofabitch." Curry had dropped his wide-lipped sneer and was spitting with rage.

Salter interrupted him, loudly, before he could continue. "Because I can assure you that if you are being followed it is not one of our men, so if you'll give me the details I'll have him picked up and we'll find out why he's following you and maybe see if we can charge him with something. What does he look like?"

It took Curry a minute to step back from the precipice of violence. Even when he did, he was still unbelieving. "Your height and build, short gray hair, blue suit—a typical cop in plain clothes."

"The car?"

"I told you, a blue Plymouth. If you are playing games with me, buddy, I should warn you I also have the number."

"Which is?"

Curry read it off a pad in front of him.

"That's not a police number," Salter said. "I'll find out who it is so you can nail his balls to your desk."

"You sure it isn't your people? Are you the only officer on the case?"

"I'm in charge of the case. I know who else is on it. No one is following you. We're too busy. I'll find out who it is."

"Just a minute. When you find out, let me know first. I may not want to pursue it."

"I'll let you know first. Then I'll put in a report. You've made an official complaint, I understand. It'll have to be dealt with. There's a file now."

"How will it have to be dealt with?"

"By me writing a report. You're not concerned, are you?"

"I've done nothing illegal, if that's what you mean."

"Then you'll want to know what I find out, won't you?"

Salter left the building and walked along University Avenue. He had already guessed who might be following Curry, and he found the car on the corner of Wellesley, parked with a view of the exit from Curry's building. He tapped on the window, and the man inside nodded to him and opened the door for him to get in.

"How's it going, Charlie?"

"What are you tailing Curry for, Dave? Who is paying your wages these days?"

"Jesus, that's quick. I'm on private business. I don't have to tell you what I'm doing."

"How long were you on the force?"

"Twenty years. Long enough for a pension."

"How are your contacts these days? Inside the force?"

"Getting thin. Most of the guys I was with have retired."

"You won't have any contacts left if you piss around on this one. We'll close you down."

"There's no need for that. This is just a little domestic problem. The usual. Why lean on me?"

"Just tell me who you're working for. I'm on a very sensitive case, Davey, old son. The guy you're following has spotted you and he thinks it's us, and he's important enough to be able to bug the chief. Anyway, I'd like to know what you're up to just in case it's got something to do with me."

"That's different. I don't see how it would, though. His wife."

"She thinks he's screwing around?"

"I guess. She wants to know where he is when he's not at home."

"How long have you been on it?"

"Two weeks."

"You'll need another legman. You're dead in the water. She'll probably pay you off now, anyway. But if she doesn't, stay in touch. Okay?"

"Sure. But this guy isn't doing a thing. She's wasting her money."

"Is she?"

"I think so. So far he's just been at work or at home."

"Something must have made her prick her ears up." Salter looked out at the traffic on University Avenue. "Where did he go last Thursday night?"

"He caught the train to Ottawa. The overnight sleeper. I had Friday off because she always met the train coming back on Friday. In fact, I took the whole weekend off. Apparently she isn't worried about him on weekends."

Salter opened the car door. "Tell her I'm on to you. You will anyway. I'm going to talk to her, but I don't mind if she knows I'm coming. If you stay on this job, talk to me, too, okay?"

"I'll tell Brearly, my assistant. He'll have to take over. Good to see you, Charlie."

SALTER DROVE BACK to his office and decided it was time to have a reassuring word with his boss, the deputy chief.

"As I said, I think they're both lying," Salter concluded. "Pickett felt the same when she was talking about how she met him at the station, and he's so keen to prove that he was out of town that I don't think it's all to get us out of his hair. But the neighbor was with her when they met the train. And he's got this letter from Ottawa. I can't go behind all that."

"Let's make sure, then leave him alone. He's a noisy bastard. What was the name of that civil servant in Ottawa?"

Salter told him.

"Phone him. Confirm that Curry was there and had a meeting. He didn't show you the letter, did he? If he says yes, forget about Curry. I think you've wandered into something between him and his wife that's making him spiky. Here. I'll do it." He picked up the phone and gave the switchboard instructions. While they waited, he said, "Sounds like the old wheelbarrow story. You know, the one about the security guards who were trying to figure out what the plumber was stealing from the construction site. Every night he left the site pushing an empty wheelbarrow. They took it apart time after time looking for a false bottom, or for stolen copper pipe in the handles. In the end they promised him immunity if he would tell them what he was stealing and how. Wheelbarrows, he said. We are trying to figure out what's wrong with his alibi, and all the time he's probably getting laid on that train to Ottawa every Thursday night. Do they have roomettes on that train? Hello, yes, sir. Toronto police here. Deputy chief. We are conducting an investigation, one that seems to touch Queen's Park, and Mr. Nicholas Curry has volunteered the information that he was with you last Friday morning and he has suggested that we confirm it with you so as to put his office outside our inquiry. No, I can't tell you that, sir. We just don't want innocent persons involved. I can't tell you that, either, sir. No, no, nothing like that. The new secret service looks after that, I understand. Just down the street from you. Yes. Yes. You did what? You are sure of that? What was his connection? He visits you regularly, I believe. And he generally goes back the same way? Friday was no different, then. Thank you, sir. Not at all. That's all we wanted to know, that he was with you Friday.'' He put the phone down and turned to Salter. "Nice work, Salter. The bastard was betting we wouldn't go behind his story. Mr. Curry met with his opposite number in Ottawa on Friday morning. The meeting ended at eleven, and then he took a car to the airport.''

"The airport?'' Salter felt stupid and angry.

"He always flies back to Toronto, always on the same flight, the noon plane to the Island Airport.''

"That gives him all the time in the world to get up to the apartment block, strangle the woman, and get back to Union Station. A breeze. Jesus Christ.''

"How would he come out at the station?''

"You ever met anyone off a train? I know, no one uses them anymore, but try it. There are two levels and about five exits, including an underground passage to the Royal York Hotel. She probably waited in the car—no, wait a minute, the neighbor waited in the car while she went inside—so she knew what ramp he came down, but it's easy to miss people. As long as he appears on time, she would have no reason to think he wasn't on the train. Time I had another word with Mr. Curry.''

''Take it easy. So he had the opportunity, but if he pulled this switch regularly, then it's still likely he had some other reason.''

''The bastard tried to dump on me and all the time he was lying. I'm going to nail his balls to his desk. My desk.''

But before Salter could leave, Pickett had returned from the apartment block with some news. He had made an identification of a picture he had been trawling around the block.

''Which one?''

Pickett opened the Ontario government staff magazine at the picture of Mr. and Mrs. Curry at the farewell dinner. ''Not him, her. One of the women in the block saw her running down the steps at about three-thirty.''

''Positive?''

''Absolutely. Her height and that hair make it pretty certain, and this old girl took a good look because she was drawing attention to herself the way she was running down the steps.''

''What the hell was she doing there?''

''Huh? Killing her old man's mistress. That's what.''

''Why?''

''She caught them on the job.''

''I don't believe it.''

"She's strong enough."

But Salter was already seeing Mrs. Curry bursting into the apartment, finding the dead girl, and running away, guessing who had killed her. He looked up to see Pickett waiting to be dismissed. "I don't think we've finished," he said. "But you can hold off until I tell you."

He felt as if they were playing solitaire and all the rows had been unlocked at once. Two, anyway. Which one should he turn over first? On the grounds that Mrs. Curry was already waiting for him after a warning phone call from her hired detective, he began with her.

THIRTEEN

SHE OPENED THE DOOR to him immediately and stood back to let him in.

"I've got another matter we have to check up on," he began. "We've received a complaint that your husband is being watched. When we investigated, we learned who was having him watched."

She had led him into the living room, where she took up her post, standing in front of the fireplace. "Who complained?"

"He did, of course."

"To the police? Why?"

"Because he thought it was us."

"He had nothing to do with that woman's death." She waved her hand, dismissing the problem. "This is something else entirely."

"He had something to do with Linda Thomas. He knew her."

"Yes, he did. And I have something to ask you about her. What business was she in?"

"She was a therapist. A masseuse."

"That all?" She had the air of a respectable woman who is about to utter an obscene word, just to let him know how far she is prepared to go to get the truth.

"Your husband was one of her clients."

"So I found out."

"Why did you have to find out? Why wouldn't he tell you? She was completely aboveboard."

"That's what worried me. I was told at first she was a tart."

"Who told you?"

"The detective I hired. The man you found watching Nicholas."

"Why did you hire him?"

"That's a stupid question. Because I suspected him. Because I found out about his masseuse, who, as I say, I assumed was a tart."

"How?"

"Never mind that. I found her name and phone number, and the detective traced her. Someone told him she was a prostitute. That frightened me. He's always chased women, usually secretaries or colleagues. I'm used to that. A tart is scary."

"Why?"

"AIDS, of course."

"So you had him followed. It didn't seem much to go on."

"I didn't have him followed until he made a mistake."

Salter waited for her to continue.

"I found out that these Ottawa trips weren't what they seemed. Two weeks ago the train was two hours late, but he was on time."

Salter pretended ignorance. "He hadn't *gone* to Ottawa?"

"He'd gone to Ottawa, all right. Oh, yes, he'd *gone* to Ottawa. But he didn't come back on the train. He came back on the plane, probably at noon. The service from the Island Airport. He could get back and have four hours before I met him at the station."

"You think he was in Toronto in the afternoon?"

"Yes. I phoned his opposite number in Ottawa on Friday. I pretended to be someone from his office here. He had already left for the airport."

"Then you knew this when I talked to you the other day."

"Yes." She lifted her chin and folded her arms across her bosom.

"You knew he was in Toronto, but you covered for him."

"After you saw him in the office—your sergeant, I mean—he came home and told me about this girl's death, and I agreed to help put you off. Then he went back to his office and came home at the usual time in case you were watching. He has a lot of explaining to do, to me. But I agreed only because, whatever else he's up to, he didn't have anything to do with that woman's death. He's not a murderer."

"Can he account for his time?"

"Not entirely." Once more she lifted her chin at Salter. "But he wasn't in that woman's apartment. I was."

All I have to do is wait, Salter thought. This job's easy.

She continued, "I wanted to catch him with her, so I went to her apartment and banged on the door. When she opened it, I barged in. Afterward I had to make up some rubbish about looking for a cat. She had no idea who I was. Nicholas wasn't there. She was with another man, drinking wine. She didn't look like a prostitute to me, by the way. Quite ordinary, really."

"She wasn't a prostitute. She was a therapist."

"Then why didn't he *tell* me?"

Salter thought he knew the answer to that one. Because Curry was afraid his wife would suspect him of looking for another kind of massage, which might have been the case.

"Who was the man she was with?"

"I don't know. Just a man."

"Could you describe him?"

"Not really. I only got one good look at him."

"Would you mind trying to put together a picture for us, an identikit? Would you come down to the station and do that?"

"Today?"

"Now. A woman was *killed* last Friday."

"Oh, all right, let's get it over with."

"I'll take you down now, if you like." If she agreed, he would be able to keep her away from a telephone until he had had his hour with Curry.

"I'll just put on some other shoes." She disappeared up the stairs and closed her bedroom door, and

Salter knew she was phoning Curry. But Curry sweating anxiously was nearly as good as Curry surprised.

AT POLICE HEADQUARTERS he waited until the technician had gotten her started on the picture, then drove to Curry's office. He could pretend not to know that Curry's wife had warned him. He could pretend to surprise him with the evidence of his guilt, with the facts of his lying.

Curry anticipated him. When Salter arrived, Curry was in his office. Standing by the window, a small, dark-haired woman was clasping her elbows, looking out at the street, and Salter knew immediately what he was going to hear.

"My wife called me. You are already aware that I was not in that apartment on Friday afternoon, so this is purely a private matter, none of your concern. Nevertheless, I'd like to settle it."

"I'm aware that your wife said that you weren't in the apartment on Friday afternoon during the thirty seconds that she was there. I'm not aware of any facts. Just what she said."

"My wife is not a liar."

"Yes, she is. She knew you weren't on the train. So far all I've had from both of you is bullshit. Excuse me, ma'am."

"What do you want to know, Inspector?" the woman asked.

"I want to know where Mr. Curry was on Friday afternoon."

"He was with me."

"And who are you?" She looked faintly familiar.

The woman flushed. "I'm fairly new to the cabinet, but I thought I was well enough known as a back bencher."

"This is Christine Fowles, minister without portfolio," Curry said.

"That should be good enough. You were together all afternoon?" He wanted to add, "looking after your portfolio?"

No one replied. "I guess we're all finished," Salter said. "Except for your complaint."

"I'm withdrawing my complaint."

"I guess you are. But I have to assure the deputy chief you won't complain again. Not about me, anyway. My career could be on the line. I'll be making a written response. Nice to have met you, ma'am."

And that, he thought, takes care of Curry. Much as he disliked the man, he had never considered him a possible murderer. He had been fairly sure for some time where to look for the killer, and he needed only to find the right road to the proof. Nevertheless, Mrs. Curry had to be eliminated first. She had motive and opportunity, and, as Pickett said, she looked strong enough. But when he got back to his office, the identikit picture she had assembled convinced him she was telling the truth.

"What did you do then?" he asked her when he saw the picture.

"I drove home. It was nearly time for me to go to the station, and I bumped into my neighbor, who offered to go with me. I went through the charade of picking Nicholas up at the usual time, as you know."

"You knew then he hadn't been on the train?"

"Yes, but I didn't know where he'd been. I'm going to find out, though."

"HE WAS IN HER APARTMENT," Salter said to Pickett later. "I've got a witness: Curry's wife. She hasn't seen this picture, but I don't have any doubts."

Then he told Pickett what he thought was going on, as much as he understood.

Pickett listened in wonder. "He was impersonating Mackane? Why? You need a theory to make sense of that one."

"I'll get that from him."

"You going to Marlborough now?"

Salter shook his head. "Tomorrow afternoon. I want you to take this picture 'round the apartment block first. I'd like to confirm Mrs. Curry's identification." He gave Pickett the group picture he had brought back from Marlborough, the picture of the sod-turning ceremony. "That's the guy. Show it to as many as you can find."

"Is Curry happy now?"

"I wouldn't call him happy, with his problems. *I'm* happy. You won't hear from him again."

"That's something. I'll see you before you go to Marlborough. You going to bring him back with you?"

"I think so. Well, sure, if you get him identified."

"What's the question? 'Did you ever see this guy?'"

"Yeah, especially that afternoon. Ask them about Mackane, too. I'm not dead certain what's been going on yet."

AFTER PICKETT LEFT, Salter checked the entries in Mackane's appointment book again. It did not take a handwriting expert to confirm that the entries that coincided with those in Linda Thomas's diary marked "Abe"—in Mackane's diary listed as "tennis"—were not in Mackane's hand. Even the ink was different.

PICKETT LEFT THE OFFICE at five and dawdled through the traffic on Yonge Street, courteously allowing everyone to go ahead, apprehensive of arriving, but whether it was fear he felt or just excitement, he couldn't be sure. He took Willis for a walk when he got home, then filled in the rest of the time cleaning up the breakfast dishes and tidying the apartment.

She arrived punctually at six, standing on the doorstep with her leather sack hanging from one arm. Pickett let her in and got her seated in the living room. "You want a cup of tea or coffee?"

"Lovely. Yes, please. Tea."

He put on a kettle and dug out a tray he had not used since his wife's death; arranged mugs, sugar, and cream; and washed out the teapot. He could hear her through the door, talking to Willis. When the water boiled, he filled the pot and took the tray into the living room, where he found her on the floor, hiding her face from the dog, who was leaping about her head, trying to lick her. She got up and sat on the couch, and the dog scrambled onto her lap.

"I can put her in the basement," Pickett offered.

"She's lovely. What's her name?"

"Willis."

The girl gave him a querying look.

"It's a joke. My wife got her name from a book."

She waited for more.

"Dickens. *David Copperfield*."

"I've read that." She shook her head, uncomprehendingly.

"Remember the carter? Wanted to marry the old nurse? I've just seen the movie."

"Peggotty," she nodded. "Of *course*. Barkis is willing. Willis is barking. What a terrible joke." She fell on Willis with glee.

"She didn't make it up. She got it from a book, another book, which had a dog called Willis in it."

"It's a lovely name, isn't it, Willis?" She butted the dog, tangling her hair in the dog's coat, sending it into ecstasy.

"So I'm the guy you're looking for. Now what?"

"You're my grandfather."

"Looks like it, doesn't it?"

She calmed the dog down and put out her hand. "I'm very glad to meet you."

Pickett felt ridiculous. They shook hands and he poured them some tea. "Now that you're here, I'm not sure it was worth coming. What can I do for you?"

"Do I look like my grandmother?"

"You are just about exactly as I remember her." The colored hair, the decorated face, concealed nothing. She even laughed like her grandmother.

"I'm not making any claim on you," she said. "I just wanted to meet you."

Pickett had been through all that in his head. "There isn't any claim. That was a long time ago."

"I won't embarrass you. I thought you said to meet me here because you didn't mind your family meeting me." She looked around the room. "If you like, though, I'll just pretend to be looking for someone else."

"I don't have any family. My wife's dead and I don't have any children. I live by myself."

"You've got Willis," she said, causing the dog to look up, ready for a romp.

"I bought her when my wife got sick. I just never got rid of her when she died."

"Does that inspector know who I am?"

I wonder, Pickett thought. "He never said anything."

"Could you tell me a little bit about my grandmother? I never knew her because my father moved away when he married. Was she nice?"

Nice. God Almighty. "Yes, she was very nice."

"Did you love her?"

"I don't know if that's the right word. I was nineteen. I think I had a crush, a big one. Later, when I saw her after the war, the crush had gone away but I still liked her. See, you couldn't say I loved her like I loved my wife."

"You came over especially to see her again, though, didn't you?"

"Not just to see her. I like England, and I used to go back whenever I could. My wife liked it, too. A couple of times, though, I went on my own and I let your grandmother know I was coming and we met in London."

"Were you still lovers? Grandmother never married. I often wondered why."

Pickett felt close to blushing. "I told you, nothing like that. We just had a drink together for old times' sake. Went for a walk in St. James's Park. Stuff like that. Nothing else. I was married."

"I wish you'd married her."

"Like I said, it would probably have been a disaster. We were never a *real* couple. I was too young for her. I just had a crush." Pickett got up and took the teapot into the kitchen and waited for the kettle to boil again. When he came back and they were waiting for the tea to brew, she asked him a question, a quiet, nervous request.

"Do you mind if I come and see you and Willis sometimes? I'm going to stay in Toronto for a little while."

"How long are you staying?"

"I'm not sure. It's a bit grotty at home, and I want to think about myself."

"You mean England?"

"Well, that, too, but I meant at our house. I can't live there anymore."

"Why? Don't you get along?"

"Daddy won't have me. He sort of threw me out. I couldn't stay away. He hit me. I hate people hitting me."

"He beat you up?"

"No, not like that. I make him angry for some reason. They're very straight, Mummy and Daddy. He's a nice man, really, but we get into arguments all the time, and the last time he hit me. Just a slap, but it was horrible."

"What does he do?"

"Work, you mean? He's an accountant, I think. He must be very good at it. We have a big house in Epsom."

"What do you argue about?"

"I'm not sure. I just irritate him. He keeps nagging me."

"Maybe he doesn't like the way you look." Pickett smiled to show it was just a mere possibility, scarcely worth mentioning.

"Why should it bother him? All my friends look like me."

"That could bother him in itself. Maybe he feels you're some kind of dropout."

"But I'm not. I have nine 'O' levels and two 'A' levels."

Pickett accepted that this was good. "Are you going to college? How old are you?"

"Nineteen. University, you mean? I haven't got a place yet. Daddy thinks I failed the interviews."

"So what are your plans?"

"I haven't any for the moment. Finding you was one plan. I like what I've seen of Toronto. Rather a sweet place. I like your cute little subway. I may see if I can find some sort of job and then when I've got some money travel some more. See the rest of Canada. My French is rather good, so I shall be all right. Do you speak French much, at work?"

"You don't get much call for it around the Bail and Parole Unit. You know, you might not find it so easy to get work. Do you have a permit?"

"I'll get something. There are always ways. I'm a quarter Canadian, aren't I? That should help."

Pickett felt the difficulty of trying to tell this brightly colored child what the real world was like, at the same time as suspecting that she knew more about the world of surviving on the fringe than he did. He thought her costume would bar her from regular employment, but he wasn't sure. He had seen enough people like her on Queen Street and the Yonge strip—weirdos, but harmless—to assume that there must be a developed subculture he wasn't aware of, a whole underground of punks buying and selling together, hiring each other, with their own restaurants, places to dance—a network.

"Where are you staying?"

"Some people I met in a shop today said they had a spare room. I have to telephone them."

"Where?"

She took a scrap of paper from her sack. "On Dundas Street. Near High Park. Is that far?"

"What kind of people?"

"Two girls. They asked me where I got my bag, and we got chatting. They share a house with some other people."

"Are you okay for money?"

"Mummy gave me five hundred dollars, and I have my plane ticket back if I get desperate."

"I have to eat supper. You want to have something with me? Then I'll drive you to this place."

"That would be lovely."

So he took her to Grano's as a place away from the neighborhood where an elderly policeman and a young girl with colored hair would attract the least attention, and they ate pizza and drank beer while he told her about himself, his life, his work, and, as far as he could construct generalizations that he didn't mind people overhearing, Canada. There seemed nothing more to say or ask about her grandmother.

Back in the house he waited until she had organized her belongings; then, overcome with a rising sense of the inadequacy of his response, said, "You can stay here for tonight, a few days, if you want. If you could manage on the couch."

She looked around the room. "Could I?"

"You'd have to put up with Willis. She sleeps up here."

She picked up the dog and sat with her in the center of the couch. "I'd love to."

"Where's the rest of your luggage?"

"It's in a locker at the bus station. But I can manage until tomorrow. I've got a toothbrush in my bag."

"Right, then. Let me show you where everything is." After a tour of the kitchen and bathroom, Pickett said, "I sleep down in the basement. You need anything else? Yeah, blankets and stuff. Hold on." He disappeared down the basement steps and came back with a pair of sheets and a duvet. "This should do you. Don't let Willis bother you. She's got a basket in the kitchen. See you in the morning."

HE WOKE UP AT FIVE and read until he heard the shower going, two hours later. He gave her another half hour, climbed the stairs noisily, knocked on the door, waited a minute, then entered the living room. Her makeshift bed was made and she was sitting on the couch with Willis on her lap, reading a paperback. "Morning, Grandfather."

"Hi. Willis! Get off there!"

Willis didn't move, just panted in his direction.

"I was reading one of your books." She held up Priestley's *Angel Pavement*. "You like cozy books, don't you?"

"What d'ya mean, 'cozy'?"

"Don't take offense. I mean big, happy-ending ones. Don't you read thrillers?"

"I tried a couple. I keep forgetting who everyone is." He changed the subject. "You look different."

The spikes were gone from her hair, which now lay in flat, mudcolored streaks. She had washed off her makeup. Now she was just a pretty girl with unfortunate hair. Pickett, used to the punk, found the new look drab.

"I was thinking about what you said about my father being irritated at the way I look. You were talking about yourself, weren't you?"

"Me? What do I care?"

"You were. And in the restaurant last night, people were staring at me."

"You must be used to that."

"Not at home. So I thought I'd try to fit in more here. I'll have to let my hair grow out. Do I look more Canadian now?"

"I guess. You look like I remember your grandmother looked."

"Do I? Good."

Pickett moved out to the kitchen and established that she had not done anything about getting herself breakfast. "What are you going to do today?" he called through the door.

She appeared in the doorway of the kitchen, the dog in her arms. "I thought I'd go for a long walk. I'll take Willis."

"She'll love that, but you might have to carry her home. I should be back around six. There's stuff in the fridge. This toast is ready. Pull those two stools out. Coffee all right?"

"Smells lovely." She sat down and put Willis at her feet. "I'll be fine. Just point me toward the high street."

Pickett thought about that. "Shops? Go out of here, turn right until you come to St. Clair, that's the high street around here, then walk west. There's about three miles of them. Maybe more."

"Which way is west?"

"To the right. You'll have to keep Willis on a leash. It's behind the front door."

He left her to clean up the kitchen and went off without even a farewell glance from the dog.

WHILE PICKETT was entertaining his granddaughter, Salter was listening to Annie.

"I spoke to Marjorie and she put me on to a villa and I called and booked it. It's near Lucca and we can have it for the third week. So we'll spend two weeks getting there and then a week coming back to Paris. Are you sure you can get away?''

"If this case isn't finished, Pickett can take over. We're through the sensitive bit. By the way, he met that girl today.''

"Does he know you've cottoned on yet?''

"We've said nothing about it, but I'm sure he does.''

Annie thought about the situation for a few minutes. "You should stay right out of the way.''

"I know. I'll try.'' He changed the subject. "What happened about the dishwasher?'' He gritted his teeth, waiting to hear that he had carefully loaded the forks into the motor.

"It was incorrectly installed,'' Annie said, keeping her face straight. "The electrician had pinched a wire under the frame.''

"I loaded it properly, then? Switched it on right?''

"The mechanic said it is foolproof. You can't set it wrong. It won't start unless you do it right.''

"Ah.'' Salter took a good drink of his beer.

"But you still have to read the manuals.''

The door burst open and Seth arrived, soaked in sweat, glasses steamed up. "Twenty-two minutes, fourteen seconds,'' he said.

"That's wonderful, son,'' Salter said. "I can see you went all out. No, don't sit down. Go and shower now. We're about ready to eat. Try not to brush against the wallpaper on your way upstairs.''

"I counted eleven," Seth said. "That includes Mr. Sandal. He was doing it on the porch."

"Doing what?"

"Smoking," Annie said. "Seth counts the number of people he sees smoking when he's running; now everyone's doing it outside. He told us about it last week. You were here."

"Ah. Well. Whatever turns you on, son." It was typical of Seth, who was rapidly turning into the moral conscience of the family. He was fiercely opposed to smoking to the point of wanting to put up a sign on the front door forbidding it in the house. He also monitored the house garbage to make sure they were recycling everything, and he was rapidly moving toward vegetarianism.

"Sandal, eh?" Salter said. "Poor bastard. He'll probably die of pneumonia."

FOURTEEN

HE SPENT PART of the morning taking around the picture that Salter wanted identified. He got lucky very quickly and drove back to the office, where Salter was waiting for him before he left.

"He's your man," Pickett said. "Three positive identifications. The guy in the Tuck Shop said he remembered him buying stuff like cans of sugared almonds. That janitor's seen him several times, he thinks, and one woman remembers him helping her when her grocery bag broke near the elevator. There's a couple of others I want to check with, chatty types who weren't around. Both of them are usually around during the day."

"Did anyone see him that afternoon?"

"The Tuck Shop guy is pretty sure, but you wouldn't want to put him in the witness box."

"I don't think it matters. Don't bother with the other two."

"I think I should. One of them is a real gossipy broad, the kind that hangs around the lobby in her slippers, looking for someone to chat with."

"Okay, but I've got what I want." Salter put on his coat. "I'm going to pick this guy up now. If you find out anything else, call me there. But only if it looks important."

"Like if someone saw him with his coatsleeves all wet?"

"That's about it."

"You want me to come with you?"

"I can manage him. He's not a roughneck. Just a liar, like everyone else in this case. If he turns funny I'll get the local boys. I want to talk to him by myself first."

"You're not satisfied, are you?"

Salter shook his head. "Let's say I'd like to keep the lawyers down to a minimum until I hear his story. It's very weird. By the way, talking of weird, how's that kid? The girl."

"The girl who came in yesterday?" Pickett asked, making up his mind. "She's at home. My place." He gave Salter time for the message to sink in. "She was looking for me." He waited for some response from Salter. "You knew that, didn't you?"

Salter shrugged and nodded at the same time, like a politician trying to remember the right gesture. "Yes, Mel, yes. Yes, I think I did."

"You were right, then." Now that it was said, the problem was Salter's. Pickett decided not to help him out.

"You're the relative?" Salter asked, eventually.

"I'm the guy her grandmother knew in the war."

"She's your—granddaughter—or something?"

"Something like that." Then, releasing Salter, he said, "I'll tell you about it later."

SALTER AVOIDED the main door at Blenheim Palace, preferring not to be noticed until he had had his talk. There was a rear door that opened into the corridor he wanted and let him dodge the president's office as he made his way to the supervisor of college services. Orchard was in his office, making out requisitions.

"Shall I close the door?" Salter asked.

Orchard looked up but said nothing.

"We have established who was with Linda Thomas on the afternoon she was killed."

Orchard closed the requisition pad and put his pencil in a drawer. "You were bound to eventually, I suppose. Shut the door or leave it open. It doesn't matter, does it?"

"I'll close it." Salter took off his coat and sat down. "So tell me. What, when, how, why. Everything."

"Where do you want to start?"

"At the beginning. With the impersonation. The first time."

"I wasn't impersonating anyone. Not really."

"What were you doing, then?"

"Enjoying myself." There was no hesitation, no spontaneity in Orchard's replies. His manner said to Salter that he had been expecting the policeman and had sorted out his story. There was no need to think about it. "I didn't think it would turn out the way it did, but once it started I couldn't see a way out. I would have looked ridiculous—to her, I mean." He cleared his throat. "I met her on a train coming back from Winnipeg six months ago."

"Just like Dr. Mackane."

"Everything I told you about her relationship with Abe was true, except that it was me, not Dr. Mackane."

"Now tell it to me again."

"I introduced myself as a college administrator, which I am. She thought I said *the* administrator, the president. I didn't correct her. It was just a bit of swank, really. I'd already told her I was at Marlborough, so when it came to names, I was Dr. Mackane. Nobody was listening. If I ever saw her again I could pass it off as a joke."

"Have you ever done this before?"

Orchard looked offended. "I'm not a real liar. Sometimes on planes and trains I've let people assume I was a professor. A lot of people do that, don't they? Like calling yourself a company director. When I was a boy, women used to say their husbands worked in business even if it was only the mail room. Human nature."

Salter said nothing. This was a confessional.

Orchard returned to his story.

"We got on too well; that's the long and short of it. By the time we reached Toronto I knew her name and number and I had asked her if I could call her when I came to town."

"As Dr. Mackane."

"I couldn't find the right way to tell her! It would have made her think I was weird. We were just having a little flirtation, I thought."

He paused. Salter nudged him along. "But it got bigger than that?"

"I thought about her a lot for the next week or so. She was the nicest person I'd met for years. Meeting her on a train like that we could be ourselves, you see."

"Except for the name and the title." The phrase slipped out like a barb, and Salter cursed his lack of professionalism. It went by without effect.

"Except for that, yes. But it was me she liked, me she wanted to be with, not Dr. Mackane. You see that?"

"You never did tell her, then?"

"It became too difficult as it went on. I had told her too many stories as Abe. And, well, in spite of what I said about it being me she liked, I was afraid she might be intrigued by my position. Abe's, that is."

"Did she ever phone you here?"

"Never. That was strictly out. She knew that I— that is, Abe—was, married and had a position to keep up, so she understood that I would do all the arranging. We were having an affair, you see." An old-fashioned man was talking about the risks he had taken for love.

"Was she used to that kind of thing?"

"No, she wasn't. She wasn't married, but she wasn't inexperienced. She'd had men friends. But I was the first married man she had known. She wasn't promiscuous."

"Were all the dates in her appointment book marked 'Abe' with you?"

"Yes. As I told you, Abe and I went to Toronto to play tennis, but I also went on my own to see Linda."

"Mackane covered for you?" It seemed unlikely.

"No, no. Everyone knew I played more often in town than he did, except that I didn't."

"You were with her the afternoon she was killed?"

"Yes, I was. We drank a glass of wine together."

"Did you fill in Mackane's desk diary while I was waiting for you?"

"You noticed that? Yes."

There was only one question left: "Why did you kill her?"

"I didn't."

"Who did? You were there."

"I know I was, but I didn't kill her. I could no more have hurt her than I could a child on the street. I loved being with her."

Strong passion evokes cliché; Salter had noticed it before, but this time he also heard the honesty, the slightly awkward shift past "I loved her" into the attempt to try to tell the truth.

Orchard continued, "I lived for those afternoons. Having someone like you that much is not all that common."

"You married?"

"Yes." Orchard stared stiffly at Salter.

"But this woman was very important to you."

"Yes. You want to know about my marriage? It's no business of yours."

Salter shrugged, staying open for Orchard to continue.

"You want me to justify myself?"

Salter said nothing.

"I suppose if I'd been honest with Linda at the beginning I might have chanced it and asked for a divorce, but I couldn't risk telling Linda afterward. She might have seen me as some kind of Jekyll and Hyde character, like a husband in one of those psychological novels where a woman wakes up and discovers she's married a monster. I doubt if I would have asked for a divorce, anyway. My wife's got a very nasty streak in her, and she might have found a way to lose me my job, and I'd never get another one like this. My wife doesn't care what I do as long as I don't rock the boat. She has her own life. She works for the municipality, she sees her sisters all the time, and she goes bowling. I put in a lot of overtime and I play a lot of sports, so we don't see all that much of each other. We're like roommates. We rub along but we don't have anything in common, nothing to talk about. The truth is, I suppose, that we don't like each other much. But it seems to suit her, and she wouldn't have such a comfortable life if I left her. We probably shouldn't have got married, but there it is."

"Why did you?"

"She needed a husband and I needed a wife, then, I suppose. Why does anybody get married?"

"Do you have kids?"

"No. You think that would have helped? That's what they say. I'm glad we haven't now. It's not what you would call a happy home."

All the time Salter was inserting his own concerns, flinching whenever Orchard said something that came close, but in the end the desert that Orchard was describing had nothing to do with him. It wasn't even a worst-case scenario. The missing element was passion—in Orchard; in his marriage; and even, Salter suspected, in his relationship with Linda Thomas. It was time to get back to work.

"Tell me what happened that afternoon. The times, especially."

"I got there about two o'clock. We talked. Drank some wine and ate some paté and biscuits. I left about four o'clock and came back to the college. I stopped off and had a hamburger because I look after myself during the week."

"What time did you get home?"

"About seven."

"You are the only person known to have been with her that afternoon. If you'd left her at five-thirty, after she was killed, you could have been home close to seven."

"I left her at four."

"Did you have intercourse with her?"

"Yes."

"Did you use a contraceptive?"

"No, I didn't."

"Did anyone see you leave?"

"I don't know. I'm sure you could find a witness if you tried. There was a woman earlier, looking for her cat."

The man was telling the truth, but Salter had a duty to the circumstantial facts. "I'd like you to come back with me to Toronto. Get your statement on paper. Do you want to phone a lawyer?"

"No. I've been through it a dozen times. You can't prove I killed her, because I didn't. I don't care how it looks."

"Let's go then. Can you walk out of here without an explanation?"

"Of course. I'm not a clerk." He straightened his desk diary, tidied some paper into a tray, and waited for a signal to move.

Salter stood up. "We'll go out the back way."

"Why?"

"Because if you're telling me the truth, then the fewer explanations the better."

"What does it matter? I'm finished around here anyway." He walked to the door.

Salter stayed where he was. "Why? Why are you finished?"

"When they find out I've been impersonating Dr. Mackane."

"How will they find out? I won't tell them."

Now Orchard stopped. "Why are you so concerned about me?" He made it seem that Salter's concern might be impertinent.

Because I'm sorry for you, Salter thought. Because you've been caught playing games, but it isn't all your fault. "Because this is a sensitive case," he said.

"Of course. Abe. I see."

On the drive back to Toronto, Salter asked, "Don't you think you might have told Linda Thomas the truth?"

"It was too big a chance to take."

Salter came to his point: "Don't you think that maybe she already knew, and didn't care? It's surprising she didn't check up on you. Most women like to be sure who they're—being intimate with."

"She understood how important it was to me—to Abe—to be utterly secret."

I wonder, Salter thought, finding it difficult to believe that Orchard would have fooled Annie for ten minutes. He found it incredible that Orchard hadn't given off some sign, some small lie that she had caught, perhaps known from the beginning. Living a double life took more training and resources than Orchard seemed to possess.

"Did you ever take her out? To a movie or a restaurant?"

"We couldn't risk that. Someone from Marlborough might have seen us."

"You could have passed her off, surely."

"That's not the point, is it? I couldn't risk someone calling me 'Tommy' while I was with her."

"I was forgetting. Didn't she ever ask you about
your work?"

"We talked about that quite a lot. It wasn't hard.
Abe used to chat to me a bit, and I knew quite a lot
about what was going on in the college."

"What about the professor stuff? What is Mackane a professor of?"

"History. I could manage that because it's always
been a hobby of mine. It would have been harder if
he'd been in something specialized, like chemistry or
mathematics, but I could carry off history. I won a
prize in fifth form for an essay I wrote on the effects
of the repeal of the Corn Laws in 1846."

"Didn't she mind that there was no future in your
affair?"

"She knew that from the beginning. She was an extraordinary woman. I'll never meet anyone else like
her." And then he talked, about her at first and about
their fortnightly trysts when "Dr. Mackane" met his
lover for two hours of pure fantasy invented to
brighten a train journey. What was it for her? Perhaps the same? An excursion into romance with the
security that it would never have to develop, never
emerge into the daylight of the ordinary world? They
were like a couple of kids, play-acting, Salter thought.

Orchard talked next about himself, about his early
difficulties in finding his feet, which made him move
to Canada. After he left school—quite a good gram-

mar school, he said, Rutland, or Rutleash, or some such name (he played rugby in the minor public schools' league)—he had clerked for several years in London. Then he was accepted into the Army and enrolled in the officers' training course, but he failed the course and had to accept reassignment as a quartermaster's clerk. He reached the rank of sergeant but left when his term was up. "I couldn't see settling down to being an NCO all my life," he explained.

He worked for ten years for a customs broker in London, doing the job well—"They pleaded with me to stay on"—but never was offered the management job he was hoping for. "There were the partners and there were the rest of us, and you couldn't cross over." In one last attempt to grab the brass ring, he emigrated to Canada.

"How old were you then?"

"Close to forty."

"When did you go to work at Marlborough?"

"Right away. I worked for a few weeks in a department store; then I saw the ad for an assistant to the supervisor of college services, and I thought I might as well have a go. I got the job at the interview and I've never regretted it."

"What was so good about it?"

"I felt at home right away. The job was straightforward enough. No problem. But it was the other things. They were just forming a rugby team when I arrived and I've always kept myself pretty fit, so I asked if they would mind if I went out to practice, and they asked me to coach the team. Same with tennis. Then after a couple of years my supervisor retired and they very decently offered me his job in spite of my lack of paper qualifications."

"Dr. Mackane give you the job?"

"No, I had it when he arrived. We became friendly when he joined a little tennis clinic I was conducting. He had been ordered to exercise for his health, and he wouldn't jog or do aerobics or anything like that. He was rusty, but he got to be a pretty fair player for his age."

"Then you met Linda Thomas."

"That's right. Then I met Linda. And now that's that, I suppose." The early shock was over, and Orchard had settled into resignation as his life unraveled fast. "How did you find out about Abe, who he was? No one knew about us, I'm sure."

Salter responded with a question: "If and when Dr. Mackane recovered enough to talk to us, you would have been found out. Did you think about that?"

"Oh, God, yes. When Abe had his stroke I thought my life at Marlborough was over, never mind when he recovered."

"Why?"

"If he'd died, there would have been an obituary, probably a picture in the *Globe,* and she would have found out who Abe was. I couldn't think straight at first. Then, when Linda was killed, I was off the hook. It was terrible, but I was almost relieved. Until you tracked Abe down."

"When I came to Marlborough first, did you know she was dead then?"

"Yes. I was surprised when you turned up because I thought you would appear right away or not at all. That's why I asked you how you found out about Abe."

"When did you hear about her?"

"Right away. Friday afternoon. Before I got back on the highway, I gave her a call—I often did that—and one of your people answered the phone, wanted to know who I was and all that, and I hung up. But I knew there was something wrong so I had the idea of phoning Mrs. Boychuck, her next-door neighbor, to ask her to give Linda a message from one of her clients. I told Mrs. Boychuck Linda's phone seemed to be out of order. Then she told me."

Such was the story Orchard believed he was telling, the story of a man indifferent to the charge of homicide but worried about being convicted of the, to him, very real crime of pretending to be Abe, like the Army crime of impersonating an officer. But Salter was listening to another story, which lay in the subsidiary clauses of Orchard's account, something he had already been made aware of by the vice president. Orchard had no idea of his real worth, of his talent for his job, learned in the quartermaster corps. He knew how things got done, what college suppliers to turn to for the small goodwill favors that were always available to important customers. When tractors were needed to haul the floats in the annual homecoming parade, Orchard arranged for them to be supplied, free, by the landscaping company that looked after the college grounds, though the college had always rented the tractors before Orchard took over. Instead of renting the grills from the gas company for the annual barbecue, Orchard instinctively borrowed them. All of this he did with his left hand, the ordinary skill of a quartermaster. Salter heard in Koren's account that Orchard had become a legend, a man who knew how things got done. He was probably, Salter thought, no more than average as a scrounger, but in the blinkered world of academe, he was the man with one eye open. Orchard and Marlborough were very happy with each other.

When Orchard fell silent, Salter asked him about Dr. Mackane.

"He's worse, I'm afraid. He won't be able to work again."

"Who's taking over? Any developments?"

"That's being decided now." Once more Orchard was standing on his ridiculous dignity. His attitude said that it was no business of Salter's.

Salter pressed on. "That vice president, you think? Koren?"

Orchard seemed to consider whether to reply. Finally he said, in a formal tone, "There was a meeting last night, and Dr. Burns allowed his name to be put forward. That means he'll get it."

Salter pushed the name around his brain. "That the eminent scholar?"

"He is eminent, yes."

"Fuzzy white hair around his ears?"

"The one you met at lunch, yes."

"Is that good? For you?" Salter asked, meaning, would Orchard still be eating at high table?

"It doesn't matter to me. When all this comes out I'll be on my way. You won't be able to keep me out of it."

"What if I can? As I said, if your story holds up, we might be able to keep your little affair in the closet. What then?"

For the first time Orchard's air of resignation cracked slightly as Salter raised the fantastic possibility that life could go on. "I don't see how you can keep it dark. But if you can, yes, I would rather work for Dr. Burns than anyone else."

"The way Koren talked to me about you, your job is safe whoever takes over."

"Is it? That's something, I suppose."

And if Dr. Burns is appointed, your place at high table is safe, Salter thought. Happy ever after.

FIFTEEN

AT HEADQUARTERS, Salter went through the motions of getting Orchard's fingerprints on record to compare with those on the wineglass. He got Orchard started on making a statement, once more warning him of the importance of calling a lawyer, but Orchard flicked the suggestion aside. As Salter was finishing with Orchard, Pickett arrived and asked permission to interrupt them. Salter stepped into the corridor.

"He was in the apartment in the afternoon," Pickett said. "The woman I missed this morning saw him. You remember I said she was the one to check." He opened his notebook. "She doesn't have any doubts. She was looking for the janitor in the corridor when she passed this guy coming out. She heard them saying good-bye. She even heard what the woman said."

Salter stopped nodding and listened hard. "Which was?"

"'Don't forget my showerhead.' He was already walking away and he turned and waved and said, 'No problem,' and the woman shut her door."

"She heard that? And saw his face? What time? What time was this?"

"Just before four o'clock. She gave up on the janitor, went back to the Tuck Shop, bought a frozen dinner, put it in the oven when she got back to her apartment, and was eating it when she heard the commotion. The dinner was a lasagna, which takes fifty-five minutes to cook and ten minutes to cool. I can testify to that."

"Is she home now?" Salter looked at his watch.

"I figured you'd want to talk to her. I told her not to go out till I called."

"Get my coat, would you? Let's get over there now."

"It's starting to look like a thief who panicked," Pickett said.

"It's starting to look like someone we know," Salter replied, ignoring Pickett's querying face. "Let me unhook this poor bastard." He went back to the office where Orchard was waiting and read through the typed statement which was ready to be signed. Then he read it again, slowly, aloud. Orchard signed it, and Salter and the attending constable witnessed it. Salter sent the constable on his way and put the statement into a file folder. Orchard sat quietly, waiting to be told what to do.

"I want to go over one detail," Salter said. "What time did you leave her apartment?"

"About four."

"What happened as you were leaving?"

"Nothing that I remember. What do you mean?"

How am I going to get this without putting it into his mouth? Salter wondered. "Did she have her clothes on when you left?"

"Of course."

"Good, you remember that. What was she wearing?"

"Her usual clothes. What does it matter?"

"I'm doing this for your benefit, Orchard. Now, concentrate on that scene in the doorway. I'll tell you if it matters or not."

Orchard looked at his feet. "A kind of brown woolly jumper—a sweater—trousers, brown slippers like dance shoes, and she had put her beads back on."

"Did she walk you to the door?"

"Yes, of course."

"Did you kiss her good-bye?"

Orchard looked down at the desk. "Yes."

"Then what?"

"Then I left."

"Did you wipe off the lipstick?"

"She wasn't wearing any."

"That's better. Then what?"

"Then I left."

"Did *you* open the door, or did she?"

Finally Orchard was concentrating hard. "I did."

"Did she hold it open?"

"Yes. I looked down the corridor, gave her one more kiss, then left."

"Did she say anything?"

There was a pause now, because Orchard's eyes were wet. A single tear ran down beside his nose and he turned away to wipe his face with a handkerchief. "As I was walking away, she said, 'Don't forget my showerhead.'"

"And you said?"

"'Don't worry, I won't.' Something like that."

"What did she mean?"

"Hers wasn't working properly and the janitor there is useless, so I said I would put a new one on for her. I'm quite handy and I did several little jobs around her apartment. I wasn't going to give her one from the stores at Marlborough, by the way. But I knew the type she needed and I planned to buy one and install it the next time I came." Suddenly, wretched, in tears, he cried out, "What *is* this all about?"

Salter let out a lot of air. "We've confirmed all this. You were seen leaving her place. She was alive when you left, and I don't think you came back half an hour later and killed her. It doesn't make any sense. I won't bother you any more if I can help it. If we catch the guy I'll still try to leave you out of it, for Mrs. Mackane's sake as much as anything. Assuming I can, you won't hear from me again. The only risk to you that I can see is if we catch the guy and his lawyers start looking for alternatives."

"Really leave me out? And Abe?"

"Really. Has anyone wondered what I came to Marlborough for?"

"Koren knows it had to do with Abe, and he tried to find out from me."

"What did you say?"

"I told him it was an inconsequential matter that the authorities had asked me to keep mum about." A hint of smugness crept into Orchard's face, still damp around the eyes.

"That's that, then. Can you get back to Marlborough all right, without anyone asking you where you were?"

"I'll go down to the club first, pick up my tennis gear, then go home on the bus. I've done that before." Suddenly Orchard looked about fourteen years old, a hero in a boys' adventure story.

"Very natural." Salter stood up and held out his hand. "All the best, Mr. Orchard."

"Thank you." Orchard blew his nose. "And thank you."

Salter watched him stride smartly past the window on his way downtown. Then he called for Pickett and they set off for the apartment block.

"THE WOMAN WHO SAW Orchard leaving, first," Salter ordered.

They took the elevator to the second floor, where Mrs. Lester opened her door as if she had been waiting behind it. Pickett introduced Salter, who asked her to come with them and show them exactly how she had seen and heard Orchard leaving. She put on some slippers and ushered them out, closing her door behind her. They moved toward the elevators.

"Oh, no!" she cried, "This way. I never use the elevators." She led the way to the other end of the hall, through a door to a fire staircase. One flight down, Salter made to reenter the corridor at the ground floor.

"I started in the basement," the woman said. "I put in a load of laundry and then came up these stairs and through here. That fellow was just walking away and I heard her ask about the showerhead. Then the door closed and I went to the Tuck Shop. Did he kill her?"

"Where did he go?"

"Out the back door, I think. Yes, because he passed the main stairs and he wasn't in the Tuck Shop when I got there. Did he kill her?"

"Did you see anyone else?"

"Only Mrs. Healy in the laundry room. Her and me had a little chat, complaining about the janitor. She was telling me he walked in on her one day without knocking. He's not supposed to do that. I told her to put her chain on and not walk around in her shift."

"Does he make a habit of walking in without knocking?"

"Not to my knowledge. Not with me." She laughed.

"All right. Thanks, Mrs. Lester."

She hovered, hoping for more, but they nodded her on her way, and Salter turned back to the janitor's apartment.

"Us again, Mr. T," he said with a noisy cheerfulness when the door opened. "I need your key for a few minutes to take another look at the apartment."

Once more the janitor protested that he wasn't supposed to surrender it, even to the police, and then he handed it over. They let themselves in, and Salter sat down in the living room and motioned Pickett to another chair. "I'm going across the hall in a couple of minutes," Salter said. "Count twenty after I'm gone, then leave here and go back to the janitor's apartment. Before you close this door, say something in the hallway, as if you're talking to someone inside. Then go along to the janitor and keep him busy for fifteen minutes. Ask him to go over the list of tenants one by one, telling you everything he knows about them. Listen to him carefully. Take notes, especially of anyone he glosses over, or claims to know nothing about. Keep him talking until I get there."

Pickett nodded, satisfied. "I thought he might be our man."

"Did you? Now we're going to find out. Count twenty, remember, and say something in the doorway."

Salter let himself out quietly and crossed the hall into the facing apartment, the apartment whose tenant still was away, as she had been before the homicide. He stood inside the door looking through the peephole. In a few seconds he heard the other door open and Pickett's voice calling, "I'll be right back." Then the door closed, and he heard Pickett's steps go down the corridor. On his hands and knees Salter searched the whole area, the hallway, the bathroom, which led off the hall, and the kitchen, which was opposite the bathroom. He found what he was looking for in the kitchen sink and around the toilet; then he found traces everywhere else. He stood up and checked the rest of the apartment carefully, not touching anything. When he was satisfied, he called his office and told them what he wanted. He was promised a team within the hour and he left the apartment, leaving the door on the latch.

It was not difficult to persuade the janitor that he was an important witness and that they had some pictures at headquarters they wanted him to look at. He fussed at first because his wife was at work and he was supposed to be available for the tenants, but this was no more than a demonstration of his conscientiousness. Salter killed a bit of time by going over the tenants' list with the janitor—Pickett had barely gotten started on it—and by encouraging the janitor to speculate about them in detail. He even persuaded him to make them all a cup of tea. After half an hour he calculated the team was on its way, and they left with the janitor for the ride to headquarters. Here the job of killing time was much easier. First Salter apologized for taking up so much of his time; then he left him in an empty office while he talked to Pickett.

"Did you notice any reaction to the tenants?" he asked Pickett.

"I thought he tried to skate past Mrs. Drummond in 704."

"How long has she lived in the block?"

Pickett leafed through his notebook. "Eight years."

"What did she say when you talked to her?"

"I drew a blank. She was the one who said she didn't know what the janitor looked like. She'd been in her apartment all day. Never saw anyone coming or going. Closed the door in my face."

"Go back and try her again. Make up a story. Ask her if she did any laundry that day. Which reminds me: Go back and try the woman in 413, too. We know *she* was doing her laundry. Find out when she went down to the basement and when she came back to her apartment, if she can remember. Find out, too, if you can, what she thinks of the janitor walking in on her without knocking. What she thinks of him generally."

Now Salter spent a bored three quarters of an hour showing the janitor pictures until the message came through that the team was finished in the apartment. He thanked the janitor for all his help and sent him on his way. Now we wait, Salter thought.

Pickett reported back by telephone. "Zero on Mrs. Drummond in 704. Still hostile. Seen no evil. Heard no evil."

"Good. What about the woman doing her laundry?"

"Nothing concrete. Very pissed off with the janitor. Says he's useless. Most of the time you can't even find him. She was looking for him in the afternoon, but he wasn't in the apartment, or he didn't answer the door. She even looked in the boiler room, but she didn't see him."

"Did you get any times?"

"She was doing her laundry from three-thirty until about four-thirty. While it was going through she tried the janitor at his apartment and then, just before she finished the laundry, she had a look in the boiler room. No sign."

"Take a look at that boiler room again. Stand in the doorway. See if you can see the chair you told me he uses, behind the boiler."

Pickett called back in five minutes. "It's not easy. There isn't much light in there. But someone at the back can sure as hell see there is someone at the door."

THE LABORATORY MADE its preliminary report the next morning, and Pickett and Salter discussed the cleanest way to break open the case.

"His wife said that he went down to the boiler room once. Otherwise he was sleeping in the apartment. She stayed in the apartment, resting, not answering the door, she said. They've cooked it up between them," Pickett offered.

"We don't have much to break them with."

"Just the lab report."

"That's evidence. I want a confession. We'll have to work on him; she's too tough. Right. Let's try it. Bring them in. Start with the Orchard bit and take it line by line. You start off, and I'll pick it up. Keep it low-key, asking for their help.''

"WE THINK WE KNOW who was with her that afternoon,'' Pickett said.

The janitor and his wife were seated side by side, opposite him. Salter stayed behind his desk, looking up occasionally. In a corner of the room, a constable appeared to be busy rearranging the pins on a notice board.

"That's a relief, then, isn't it?'' Mrs. Turnow responded immediately, looking at her husband. Turnow looked nervous, shifting his hands about his thighs, but he also nodded.

"We want you to take a good look at the picture here. You've seen it before, but now try to remember every time you ever saw him.'' He showed them the picture of Tommy Orchard.

"That's him,'' Mrs. Turnow said. "He's been in and out a lot. One of her regulars.''

"Yeah,'' Turnow agreed, looking slightly less anxious. "I've seen him.''

"There's a problem, though. We know she was alive when he left her about four o'clock. He's been positively identified as the one who left her about that time. And we know he didn't come back.''

Turnow opened and closed his mouth several times. His wife watched Pickett closely. Pickett continued, "We think he might have gone down to the basement, though, and come back through the fire door.

That way no one would have seen him." He spoke confidingly, soliciting their assent.

"Likely," she nodded. "Of course." She nodded again, this time staring at her husband until he nodded, too.

Pickett looked at Turnow. "When you went down to the boiler room, did you notice anyone around?"

Turnow picked up a look from his wife. "Not that I remember."

"Did you see anyone in the laundry room?"

"I may have. I didn't see him, though."

"There were two women doing their laundry then. One of them had been looking for you. She didn't see you go by."

The janitor looked as if he were going to burst.

"She kept her eye on the boiler room, too. She didn't see you there, either."

Mrs. Turnow looked at the three officers in turn. "Don't say any more, Larry. They're trying to trick you. They know something. Don't say another word."

"I didn't go near her apartment. Nowhere near."

"Don't say any more, Larry. Someone saw you coming out of her place."

"Who? What are you talking about?" He turned around to face her. "What's your fucking game?"

"Keep your mouth shut, Larry. Somebody saw you. This is all a trick."

"Nobody saw me, not near her apartment, not coming out, nor in the goddamn boiler room." Turnow was staring at her now, ignoring Pickett.

"Somebody might have heard you."

"How the fuck could they? I wasn't there."

"Shut your mouth, Larry."

"You weren't in your apartment, either, were you, Larry?" Salter said.

Slowly Turnow shook his head. "No, you're right. I wasn't in my apartment, either. We made that up."

"Shut up, Larry."

"Why, Larry? Why did you make it up?" Pickett asked.

"She thought we should account for each other like we did. I didn't want to tell her where I really was, so we made that up. Alibis, like. But I wasn't in that woman's place and I wasn't in no boiler room."

"You goddamn *were!*" she screamed. "I heard you!" She turned to Pickett. "I heard him. He was in there, up to his old tricks. I heard him."

"What did you hear?"

"I heard him tell her he'd fix her shower. He was in there, all right."

Pickett looked sadly at Turnow. "That night, Larry?"

Turnow swiveled and focused squarely on his wife. "I don't know what all this about the shower is. I was nowhere near that apartment. From one o'clock until past five I was on the seventh floor, with Mrs. Drummond."

Pickett watched Mrs. Turnow take in this new development. It took several seconds, then she burst: "You bloody liar!" she screamed. "I *heard* her asking you to fix her showerhead as you walked down the corridor."

Now his rage consumed Turnow, and before anyone could intervene he brought his fist around in a colossal swing, catching her on the side of the face, knocking her out of the chair and onto the floor. They were on him immediately, but there was no follow-through. Pickett helped the woman up and sat her back on her chair.

"Goddamn bitch," her husband said. "You killed her, didn't you? You thought I was screwing her. That was what that was all about when I came in. You didn't want me to go over there, did you?" He turned to Pickett. "She was soaking wet when I came in. Washing out the bathtub, she was. I thought that was funny; that's my job. Then she tries to stop me going across the hall. When I came back she cooks up this bullshit about me and her being asleep so we'd have alibis. I went along with it so she wouldn't ask me where I'd been. You can ask Mrs. Drummond. She'll tell you. I was with her all afternoon."

"Shut your mouth, Larry."

"All afternoon. I bin seeing her regular for a few months now. We're lovers. All the time you thought I was seeing Miss Thomas I never went near her. Didn't have to. I had Mrs. Drummond." He turned to Pickett. "I thought she'd done it, couple of days after. You can tell, can't you? She was acting strange. Being nice."

"You bastard."

"Me? I din't kill no one. I was just with Mrs. Drummond. Not hurting no one."

"I didn't kill her." Mrs. Turnow was recovering slightly.

The show was over. "Take him into the other office and get a statement," Salter said to Pickett. "And get one from Mrs. Drummond. Now, Mrs. Turnow, I'm going to charge you formally with the death of Linda Thomas. You don't have to say anything. Call your lawyer. Then I'll tell him where you were at four o'clock on Friday and what you were doing."

"I'VE GOT A STATEMENT," Salter said later. "It's probably going to be manslaughter. She still doesn't believe it wasn't her husband who left the apartment at four. But finding out about Mrs. Drummond unhinged her."

"Who else but the janitor fixes showers?" Pickett asked rhetorically. "Though living with him she might have known that her husband couldn't fix a light bulb, let alone a showerhead."

"You put me on to it when you told me about the apartment opposite. It's not in line with the one across the hall, so she couldn't see who was leaving. What she heard Linda Thomas say was enough. She stewed around, scattering cigarette ashes all over the floor, leaving her prints all over the doorjamb, until she couldn't stand it. She didn't even knock. She had the master key, so she just charged in and found Linda Thomas getting ready for a bath. Then she saw the wine and glasses. She didn't plan to kill her. She got in a rage and went for her throat. Banged her head against the wall—a bit too hard. Then she panicked and pushed her into the tub, then opened a door onto the balcony to make it look like an outsider. When Turnow found the body she persuaded him it'd look suspicious, that we might try to nail him for it, the police being what they are, and it would be best to cover each other with a story so they could stay right out of it. Don't forget she thought he had been in the apartment and might have been seen. She planned to stick him with it if she had to. He went along with her because he didn't want to explain where he'd spent the afternoon, which she wasn't pressing him about because she thought she knew."

"She was hoping to keep them both out of it?"

"That's right. She wasn't going to stop him unless it came to a choice between the pair of them. Then she was. She knew, or thought she knew, that either one of them might have been seen in the corridor so she invented the two little errands, him down to the boiler room all afternoon, but she persuaded him it would look better if they said they had both been home all the time. Liars, the lot of them."

"Was that all you had to go on? That you couldn't see across the hall from one apartment to the other? You took your chances, didn't you?"

"That and the smoking. You saw that sign in the apartment? When I looked around the first time you could still smell it. Smoke. Then my kid came home the other day from running and told us how many people he'd seen smoking outside. That's what triggered me off. Mrs. Boychuck looked after her plants but she didn't smoke; I didn't remember Turnow smoking, but his wife's a chain-smoker. She'd spent a lot of time in that place. You didn't need a magnifying glass to see the ashes all 'round the toilet bowl. Anyway, I didn't accuse her until the lab came up with her fingerprints. I've got her statement now before she'd had time to realize that, as the janitor's wife, it's only natural she should have been in there from time to time, making sure everything was all right.''

SIXTEEN

WHEN PICKETT CAME HOME that afternoon he found his sister-in-law and nephew sitting in his living room. "How did you get in?" he asked.

Verna pointed toward the kitchen, a large, sharp, peremptory jab, as if she were poking a hole through a screen. "She let us in."

In the kitchen, Imogen was sitting on a stool, reading, Willis on her lap. "She says she's your sister-in-law," Imogen said. "I offered to make tea, but she said if she wants tea she will make it herself. They won't talk to me."

Pickett returned to the living room and sat down. "How's everything, then?" he asked. He started to unlace his shoes.

"What's going on, Mel Pickett?" Verna responded.

"Not too much. I've just finished a case. Might take a couple of days off." He undid his tie and rolled it into a snake.

"Her, I mean. Who's that?"

"Imogen Colwood her name is. Didn't she introduce herself? She's staying here. With me."

"You getting senile in your old age?"

"How do you mean?"

"Bit young for you, isn't she?" the boy asked. "More my age."

"You think so?" Pickett felt the gates opening and a lovely flood of rage pour through his veins. Just a bit more, he thought. Hang yourself.

"It's a desecration of my sister's memory."

"How do you mean?"

"Taking a cheap tramp into her bed."

"Is that what I'm doing?"

"What else?"

"I'd have thought you were a bit past it," the boy said.

"That's enough, Harvey," his mother said. "Where did you find her? On Jarvis Street?"

Now? he wondered. Yes, now. "She's my granddaughter."

Perfect. Verna rose from the couch and moved forward as if a large spike had been thrust into each buttock. "She's *what?*"

"She's my granddaughter."

"What are you talking about?"

"Imogen!" Pickett called through into the kitchen. She came as far as the door, cradling the dog in her arms. "This is my sister-in-law, your great-aunt Verna, and her son, Harvey. This is my granddaughter, Imogen Colwood." It was like the end of one of his favorite novels.

Verna jerked around as if the spikes were being twisted, turning to her son, then to the girl, and back to Pickett. "What are you up to?" she demanded.

Having got all the response he could have hoped for, Pickett relaxed a little. "Seems I left a kid behind when I was in the Air Force in England. Imogen's father. Imogen just caught up with me last week."

"She came here to find you? After forty years?" She stared at Pickett, then at her son, looking for him to equal her disbelief.

Pickett looked at Imogen. "Yes," she said.

Verna kept her eyes on Pickett. "I don't believe it," she said. "I never heard of any kid in England."

"I didn't tell anyone. You didn't in those days."

Verna subjected the girl to a long, quivering stare. "How do you know this kid is yours? How can anyone tell?"

"She's the image of her grandmother. I recognized her as soon as I saw her." He looked at Imogen warmly.

"How long is she staying?" She turned back to the girl. "How long do you think you're staying?"

The girl opened her mouth to speak, but Pickett got in first. "She might settle here. She's going to sleep on the couch until the students leave upstairs. Then she'll move up there." He felt Imogen's face turn toward him, but he was afraid to look up.

"But that's where my Harvey's going."

"Yeah," Harvey said, slightly animatedly. "That's where I'm staying."

"Sorry, old son. You'll have to find somewhere else."

"Somewhere else!" Verna screamed. "Somewhere else! I'm not having that. Harvey's staying here. She'll have to find somewhere else, not him. That flat is his."

Pickett found it hard to believe she was saying these things, that she would go this far, but she was out of control. That she was saying them, however, released him from the need for courtesy, took away any shred of obligation to her. "There was never any question of Harvey staying here," he said. "Not for a minute."

"But you said—"

"I didn't say nothing. You did all the talking."

"He's your nephew."

"I know, and I'm tired of being reminded of it. So I'll tell you this: For Mary's sake, if ever he becomes destitute or you do, call me and I'll make sure you don't want for the essentials. In the meantime, I'd just as soon leave it at that. Let me know if you're in bad need, Verna. You too, Harvey. In the meantime don't come around anymore. Either of you. We don't like each other, and I don't owe you anything."

"Jesus Christ!" Verna yelled, shocking Pickett, for she was a churchgoing woman. "Come on, Harvey. I'm going to get to the bottom of this."

"Let me know what you find there."

"I don't think she's your granddaughter at all, Mel Pickett. I think you've got the hots for a little tramp, that's what I think, and you're making this all up just to cover up. You're not fooling me, or you either, you little bitch. You're a dirty old man, Mel Pickett. All your brains have gone to your—"

"Out!" Pickett ordered. "Out, out, the pair of you! Here's your coat. Here's your purse. Harvey, take her things. Now. Out. Go on. Go." He closed the door sharply behind them, leaving the pair in disarray on the porch. He watched them through the window shouting at each other on the sidewalk until Harvey finally bundled her into the car, still shouting.

THE GIRL WAS STILL standing at the door of the living room, holding the dog. "I've caused a lot of trouble. Should I go?"

"She's really something, isn't she? No, don't worry about it. It's been coming for a long time. Now let's eat."

"I got the stuff to make spaghetti. Is that all right?"

"That's great. Anything we need? Bread?"

"I've got everything. Do you want to eat your dinner right away? Or do you have a bath or a drink or something first?"

"The bath can wait, but I need a drink."

"I bought some wine in a store near the underground station. It's Canadian."

"A beer is what I need. Two, probably. You have wine."

She put water on for the spaghetti and they walked out to the back porch, where it was sunny, if chilly, and watched Willis run around in circles.

"Did you mean that about the flat, or was that just a way of getting rid of your nephew?"

"It was the easiest way of getting rid of him." And then the marvel struck him again, the sheer delight at having her around for whatever length of time she stayed, and he realized how close his feeling was, without actually being that feeling, to what his sister-in-law had assumed. "But I did mean it. Stay if you like. Until you decide what to do."

"I want to stay in Canada. I knew that after two days. Could I live here, just for a little bit?"

"Until you get tired of it. As long as you like. Now let's eat."

AFTER DINNER, in response to a question from Pickett about what she planned, or would like, to do, eventually, she said, "What I'd *really* like to do is get into radio or television. It's almost impossible, I know, but that's what I'd like to do."

"You want to talk to someone about getting in over here? I think I could fix that."

"*You* could. Who?"

"Guy I know. Friend of mine. TV host. He'll do it for me."

"That would be marvelous. Is this someone you arrested once?"

"They aren't all villains, the people I know."

"I'm sorry. It really is a small country, isn't it?"

"Smaller than that. Something else I could try. You really want to stay here? Work? Immigrate here?"

"I'd like to, but even having a grandfather here doesn't give me enough points. I would have to go back to England and apply and wait, I think."

"Let's find out. I know a guy who knows people in Ottawa."

"Ottawa?"

"The government. I'll give him a call. Find out if there are any exceptions."

"The rules are very clear."

"It won't hurt to find out if they plan to rewrite the rules in the near future. There's an election coming up." He changed the subject. What he planned to do was something he was against in principle, like fixing traffic tickets, but he was in a mood to cash in all his credits to keep her around. She didn't have to know. "This weekend," he said, "you'll have to look after the house. I'm going up to start work on a cabin I'm building."

"You're building a cabin? What kind?"

"Yeah. About a hundred and fifty miles north of here. A log cabin."

He explained it to her then. Explained the principles of log construction, told her about the site, about his little trailer, and about how this weekend he was going to lay his first four, perhaps eight, maybe even twelve logs. "I probably won't use it once I've built it."

"That's wonderful. It's like, like all the stories. Can I come?"

It hadn't occurred to him, but as soon as she asked, he could think of nothing he would like more. "The flies will be bad," he said. "And it's only an itty-bitty trailer, but it'll be okay for a night."

"I could do the cooking, couldn't I? Does Willis like it?"

"She loves it. Spends her time barking at the otters in the pond."

She turned and wrestled the dog to the ground. "We're going up to the cabin, Willis," she said, making the dog bark in glee.

The next day Pickett phoned Fred Doughty and made the first deal: He would explain the police to Doughty, take him on a tour of headquarters, arrange for him to spend a night in a squad car, if Doughty would see what he could do for the girl, show her how to get a foot in the door. Then with Salter's permission he telephoned Curry and explained that they had been able to submit the simplest of reports on Curry's complaint, dismissing it as a domestic incident, so that all Curry had to be concerned with was his wife. No names would be raised, either verbally or in writing.

"Thank you, Sergeant."

Then Pickett explained what he wanted Curry to do for him. He was not surprised when Curry immediately responded, for openers, that what he wanted was irregular, possibly illegal, probably impossible, that the rules were very strict, that priorities had to be observed. He simply waited until Curry moved on to saying that, however, since there was no real quota, no one could be hurt, she certainly had compassionate grounds—estranged from her parents, was she? grandfather her only responsible relative—and that he did know someone in Ottawa he'd been helpful to in the past, and then, though he went back on track once ("all I can do is bring the name to his attention, make sure her application is given a proper hearing"), Pickett understood that he would get what he wanted. He put the phone down feeling like Mr. Big.

AFTER CORRUPTION, mendacity. Three days later, Salter invited Pickett and his granddaughter to supper. This was not a rare case of Salter socializing with one of his colleagues; Annie was intensely curious. The excuse was that in the absence of any women around Pickett, Annie might be able to advise the girl about Toronto.

The arrangements had involved a long discussion about whether they should eat in the handsome new kitchen or in the dining room. The dilemma had been heightened by a visit from Salter's father who, on being invited to eat Sunday dinner in the kitchen, had asked them who they were saving the dining room for, royalty? Annie wanted to show off the kitchen, but Salter didn't want Pickett to feel he was eating with the servants. The problem was solved by Annie insisting they have their predinner drinks in the kitchen so that she could talk to them while she cooked, and then, at the point at which she ought to have been setting the dining-room table, exclaiming, "Why don't we stay in here. It's hard to talk with just four of us around that table."

It was a ridiculous reason, but Salter, watching the mild expression of approval and relief flit across Pickett's face, gave in.

The supper was a success. Afterward Imogen and Annie stayed in the kitchen talking, while Pickett and Salter watched a hockey game on television.

When they had gone, Annie said, "A nice kid, never mind the gear, but I don't think she's his granddaughter."

"How do you know?"

"She has nothing of him. Nothing. Body shape, eyes, skin, nothing. She comes from a different race."

"He says she's just like her grandmother."

"I don't doubt it."

"You think he's being conned?"

"I don't know. He admitted he was her father's father, didn't he?"

"That's what he told me."

"I don't think he is."

"Shall I tell him you said so?"

"Don't be silly."

"You think he knows?"

"That, as they say, is a good question. If he does, he's got a secret, hasn't he? How old is he, by the way?"

"About sixty-three. Why?"

"Will you be like that in ten years?"

"What do you mean?"

"You're a lot like him now."

"What are you talking about?" Salter felt his uniqueness threatened. "He's about seventy pounds heavier than me. Why? Would you mind?"

"Not if we were building a log cabin. He's nice. Now, about this vacation. I want to see Provence. Everyone says it's special. We'll go to Nice and then turn north."

"As long as we go to Monte Carlo. I want to see the casino and the nudist colony." Then he made a dive for her, rumpling her fiercely in a mock attempt to undress her as he vented his real need to give physical expression to his relief that she was back. They could talk later.

When Seth came home a few minutes later from a visit to a friend he found two disheveled parents on their hands and knees on the living room floor, apparently searching for one of Annie's earrings.

The next day, as they were finishing up the case, Salter said, "She seems like a nice kid, Mel."

"Yeah? She enjoyed meeting your wife last night. I did, too. She's a very classy lady. Nice to see a really solid couple in this business. What's the secret?"

"Just luck, I guess. But your granddaughter. She doesn't take after you, does she?"

"No?"

"You'd never know she belonged to you."

"Say it," Pickett commanded.

"You sure she's who she says she is?"

"She's her grandmother's granddaughter, no doubt about that."

"Yeah, but is she yours?"

"I admitted it once already."

"But could you have been wrong? How well did you know her?"

"Too late for that now."

"You feel responsible for her."

"While she's here, sure."

And that was as far as Salter got, for there was no doubt in Pickett's mind, as there had not been in 1945, when Olive Colwood had come to him in terror. He had been in love with the girl for months; she was the chief constituent in his Anglophilia, and they had spent a lot of time together. He was always aware, though, of someone in the background whom he must not ask about, someone who left her with enough time for Pickett, someone, nevertheless, she was in love with. She had made this clear when Pickett had tried to come too close, and he had waited and waited for the situation to change, for the ghost to disappear. Instead she had become pregnant, but not by Pickett, who returned to Canada as virginal as he had left.

When she came to him he was appalled, but she needed help that only he could provide. Her lover was a civilian, married, a neighbor on her street in Croydon. In 1945 there was no room for a man in his position, lower-middle-class, a teacher of art in a secondary school, unfit for war service, to have an affair with a girl in the WAAF. If he left his wife he would never get another job; divorce took seven years, and besides, he did not want a divorce. She was in love, as Pickett was with her, but the art teacher was just being a little bohemian, playing a role, and he had no desire to abandon everything for a pregnant Olive Colwood.

Her father had to be faced. He, too, was lower-middle-class, respectable, a clerk in the town hall, and a savage tyrant at home. A cliché. He demanded to confront the father and have it out with him, and Olive doubted her ability to resist him. He would wear her down eventually. She talked to Pickett endlessly, trying to find a solution, but when he came to the answer she rejected it immediately before he had made it clear what he was proposing. He would not marry her. (He would have, but she wouldn't hear of it.) What he proposed was to admit to being the father and refuse to marry her.

The next few weeks were both hellish and enormously satisfying for the young romantic Pickett. His station commander treated him with a mixture of contempt (at being a fool for admitting paternity) and irritation (for causing him—the commander—so much trouble). The father was as outraged as Olive had predicted, storming down to Bournemouth, demanding justice in the form of a marriage for his daughter, confronting Pickett, calling him names ("Yankee sex maniac" was his favorite) and finally, as they had hoped, turning with increased sympathy to his poor, betrayed daughter when he found himself up against the refusal of Pickett to be moved by her condition or anything her father could say. Olive was demobilized and had her baby at an aunt's in the country, where the story was put about that her fiancé had been killed in a flight over Germany. Even the lower middle class could not look too harshly on such a tiny lapse of morality in wartime, and she raised her child in peace.

Pickett closed the file on Linda Thomas and looked up at Salter, on the brink of confessing the greatest story of his life. If I don't tell him, he thought, I'll look like a sucker, being conned again, as he thinks I was forty years ago. But if I do tell him, what will he think of me, young Galahad as I was then? And then there's the kid, Imogen. Fuck him, he thought. What do I care what he thinks?

"Anything else?" he asked. "If not, I guess it's back to Bail and Parole for me." He laid the file on Salter's desk. "If you get any more sensitive cases, you know where to find me. If Taffy Williams can spare me."

DEADLY PROMISE

MIGNON F. BALLARD

You'd better watch out,
You'd better not cry,
Or there's no doubt
You're the next one to die...

The first victim was her husband. Then his best friend. So Molly Stonehouse had come to Harmony, Georgia, for Christmas—to discover who in her husband's cheery hometown was a murderer.

At the center of the mystery is a secret from the past, an innocent, boyish prank that, decades later, is unfolding with deadly precision.

 WORLDWIDE LIBRARY
TM

HAL'S OWN MURDER CASE
LEE MARTIN

LABOR PAINS

Two weeks away from the birth of her baby, Ft. Worth detective
Deb Ralston decided her sixteen-year-old son, Hal, had picked a rotten
time to hitchhike halfway across the state with his girlfriend, Lorie, and be
arrested for murder.

The victim, a young woman, had been hacked with Hal's hunting knife
and left in Lorie's sleeping bag. Now Lorie is missing and Hal's in jail.

Ralston hits the tiny East Texas town in her official capacity as worried
mother—a role that quickly expands into investigating officer. The trail
leads to places of the heart no mother-to-be wants to go...but with a cop's
unerring instinct, she follows the ugly path into the twisted mind of a
ruthless killer.

 **WORLDWIDE LIBRARY**
TM

Flight to
YESTERDAY
VELDA JOHNSTON

A NIGHTMARE REVISITED

Dubbed a "young Jean Harris" by the press, Sara Hargreaves spent four years in prison for a crime of passion she didn't commit. Now she's escaped, and she's desperate to clear her name and to see her dying mother.

As her face appears nightly on the local news, Sara disguises herself, and with the help of a young law student she is forced to trust, she returns to the scene of the crime.

The fashionable sanatorium where handsome plastic surgeon Dr. Manuelo Covarrubias was stabbed with a knife bearing Sara's fingerprints looks much the same. But as Sara begins her flight to yesterday, the secrets surrounding the callous playboy doctor who jilted her unfold. Secrets that once drove someone to murder...secrets that could kill again.

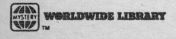

Can you keep a secret?

You can keep this one plus 2 free novels.

THIS BLESSED PLOT

M.R.D. MEEK
A LENNOX KEMP MYSTERY

Rich and poor. Lennox Kemp knew they all had their peculiarities. On the other side of the tracks—although disguised behind fine crystal and patrician smiles—were the Courtenays.

Twins Vivian and Venetia were rich, reckless and probably quite ruthless. They needed Kemp to oversee the legalities of the rather bizarre plans for their massive inheritance....

"M.R.D. Meek moves ever closer to the charmed company of Ruth Rendell and P. D. James."

—*Detroit News*